Books by Skoot Larson

# The Lars Lindstrom Zen Jazz Mystery series

The No News is Bad News Blues

The Real Gone Horn Gone Blues

The Dig You Later Alligator Blues

The On the Road Again Blues

# The Dave Holman "Texas" Mystery series

The Texas Detective

The Pachyderm Predicament

The Ivory Coast Puzzle

# Humor

Apollo Issue, a Humorous Look at Healthcare

The Palestine Solution

The Testament of Jessica Crystal

King Irv's Big Adventure

King Irv's Cabernet Caper

# FRIEND

## A Political Fable

Skoot Larson

Skoot's Jazz Books

ISBN: 978-0-692-89762-1

Published by Skoot's Jazz Books

Rockport, Texas

To my brother, Jim Larson. Thanks for a lifetime of friendship and sharing books, and to Mary and Jim Senior, our parents, who always stressed the importance of reading and learning.

And again. thanks to my editor, Theresa Feeser for her excellent work.

**May 3, 2016, a day that will live in infamy...**

Out beyond the coral reef, Margo noticed a ship heading for the harbor of the small, unspoiled island of Santa Nepenthe. "Do we have a delivery scheduled today?" she asked Sport, the man behind the bar in the island's waterfront tavern. Without looking up from the margarita he was mixing, Sport replied, "Wednesdays and Fridays. The supply ships from Puerto Rico come on Wednesdays and Fridays. You should know that by now."

Margo ordered another Piña Colada, sipped it slowly, and stroked the tabby cat that sat in front of her on the bar top as she watched the approaching gray vessel. She ordered some boiled local shrimp as the vessel neared the dock. Margo was running her last shrimp through the cocktail sauce when the ramp was brought from the vessel's deck and green clad soldiers began to pour forth onto the wharf led by an overweight man in a white ice cream suit and dazzling Panama hat. The soldiers, carrying nasty looking machine pistols, quickly fanned out along the waterfront.

Sensing a story, Margo fished through her purse for her old press credentials. She rushed out the door and ran up to the man in the white suit. "Margo Drelve, New York Tribune," she shouted, half out of breath. "Can you tell me what's going on here?"

With his nose in the air and a condescending glare in his piggy eyes, the man replied, "Isn't it obvious? We have come to build the airport."

"With soldiers?" Margo asked in a confused tone.

"The soldiers are only here to conscript laborers," the man replied.

"But they haven't held the island's elections yet," she cried. "The people may not *want* an airport. We won't know until the people have spoken."

"There will be no elections," the white clad man told her.

"And you're *conscripting* labor, not hiring them?"

"When the airport plus a hotel and casino are up and operating, bringing in a profit, we will consider *hiring* some of the brightest and most loyal," he told her. "As for now, our idiot friend running for the office of island leader here has given away too much of my money but produced too little in the way of positive support for our project."

"But the labor will be paid?" she asked with a voice full of concern as she scribbled quick notes on her spiral bound pad.

"They will be fed and sheltered. That is all I can promise until the casino brings us a profit." With that, the man turned back toward his troops signaling that the interview was finished.

# Part I

# 13 months previous…

"**S**o where in the hell is Santa Nepenthe and why would anyone in their right mind want to go there?"

Margo's editor, Geophrey, was leaning over into her face, supported by his straight locked arms and knuckles that rested halfway across her desk. His face looked angry, but then Geophrey's face always looked angry. As the senior editor of a mid-sized New York daily, Geophrey was constantly up against deadlines as well as pressure to stay on top of whatever was happening in the world. Margo expected him to have a stroke or a major coronary at any time but the man just seemed to thrive on the pressure, tempered by a fair bit of gin and very little rest. If anyone had newspaper ink flowing in his blood it was Geophrey Harrison.

"Geoph," she smiled at him rolling her chair back slightly to reclaim some of her personal space, "you know I've been trying to write the great American novel for as long as I worked for the Trib. But it just isn't going anywhere."

"Yeah, right," her boss answered. "Every junior reporter I ever met is writing the great American novel…"

"Geoph, I'm serious. I know I've got at least one best seller in me, I *know* it, but I have to get away to someplace quiet where I can think. I'm only asking for a year's sabbatical."

"The sabbatical isn't a problem. You're a crackerjack journalist and we want you back here at the Trib when you've had your time off. I'm just questioning what you think you're doing."

"Well, I want to go someplace tropical, with a beach and lots of sunshine… but I don't want to be somewhere with tons of tourists and beach bums distracting me. Santa Nepenthe hasn't really been discovered by the cruise-ship crowd yet. It's supposed to be very laid back and quiet."

"So where the hell is this place?"

"It's in among the Virgin Islands. The British have some of the Virgins and the Americans took over the islands that had been claimed by Denmark. Santa Nepenthe was originally claimed by the Portuguese, but later fell to the British, so it was one of the British Virgin Islands, but the English crown didn't see anything of value there, so they granted it a sort of independence. The island doesn't even have an airport. I'm going to have to fly into San Juan, Puerto Rico, and take a supply ship to Cidade Sebastian, the westernmost port city." Margo didn't mention that it was the island's *only* port city or for that matter the only center of population that could even remotely be regarded as a city. "I figure it will be peaceful and distraction free, the perfect place to think and write."

"If you don't start hallucinating from boredom. Why not the south Texas coast or somewhere on the Mexican Caribbean? Someplace where you can at least check facts on the Internet."

"I wrote to the Souza government on Santa Nepenthe to get my visa. They told me the entire island has free Wi-Fi access to the Internet. It's provided by the government. It might be third world, but it sounds like they treat their citizens *very* well."

"I don't know," Geophrey scoffed. "It sounds like trouble to me. I wouldn't want to touch the place with a barge pole… but it's your life, sweetie."

Margo smiled. "I have a good feeling about the place. I just know I'll return with a publishable work that everyone will want to read."

# Chapter One

It was thirty degrees and snowing as Margo's Air Americas flight sat on the runway at Newark, New Jersey, waiting for the truck that could de-ice their wings. Her phone told her that it was in the eighties in St. Thomas, only sixty or so miles from Santa Nepenthe. There was no weather station on her small island destination so St. Thomas was as close as she could get for a fix. Margo read through her notes again as she waited. She had her passport, her visa papers printed off the Internet, and her reservation at the Sovereign Hotel in Cidade Sebastian.

The Sovereign had given her a special six-month rate, less than half the nightly or weekly tariff. They hadn't mentioned that the hotel had a year-round vacancy rate of over ninety percent. They also hadn't mentioned that fresh water was iffy, depending on how much rain fell in the area, Santa Nepenthe having no source of water beyond what fell from the skies, or that their staff only showed up to work when they felt like it.

Margo's flight departed only four hours late, the crew concerned about a tropical depression in the northern Caribbean. The trip took longer than expected as the airline went west toward Mexico and then east to their destination, avoiding large thunderheads moving through the Bahamas. They touched down in San Juan, Puerto Rico seven hours late, which caused Margo to miss the Thursday supply boat to Santa Nepenthe. The customer service desk for Air Americas arranged a room at a cheap hotel on the Condado, close to the El Morro fort and the city beaches. "You'll have some wonderful sightseeing in the area," the lady at the desk told her with a broad, false smile.

Margo stayed in her room through the week end. She sat at her laptop and ate room-service food, mostly bad hamburgers and fish stews, while she revised the plot for her book. It was a mystery with political overtones, dark and violent. Her projected characters were to be bent policemen, a crooked politician and assorted big moneyed interests, but all she could think about was airlines that couldn't keep a schedule and their public relations apologists. God how she wished that she was already in her quiet tropical paradise, far away from these twenty-first-century whackos. She knew that if she was in Santa Nepenthe the story ideas would be flowing almost too fast for her to keep up on her computer.

With the onset of writer's block, Margo started hitting the tiny bottles in the hotel's mini-bar. By Monday night, she was having trouble finding the bathroom in her hotel suite. Tuesday morning she woke up late with a terrible headache and almost missed the 9:45 supply boat to Santa Nepenthe.

With no time to grab breakfast, she dragged her bags up the gangplank only minutes before the captain pulled the old rust-bucket, the MV Dexter, away from the dock. Looking around her, Margo marveled that this rusting tub was still afloat, let alone making weekly trips to the outer islands.

They crossed over choppy seas and arrived at the long concrete block jetty of Cidade Sebastian just after three in the afternoon. No one was there to meet or greet them and there was no taxi in sight so Margo carried her bags down the long cement wharf to the shore. At the shoreline, where the pier became a boardwalk of weathered wood, Margo glanced up at the flag fluttering from a pole so rusted that brown flakes of the metal fell in the light breeze. The banner was divided diagonally from the upper right corner to the bottom left; the top panel was bright scarlet and the bottom dark blue. In the center of the cloth a seagull was perched on a light brown gourd.

Across from the harbor and behind the flag pole, Margo noticed an old stone building with moss hanging along its outer walls and a fading yellow sign that said 'Bar.' A small troop of what appeared to be feral cats were camped out along the old stone walls. The structure also had a faded blue placard indicating the presence of a public telephone.

Margo decided that this might be the place to inquire about a taxi to her hotel and have a little libation while she waited. She dragged her bags through the wide doors, found her choice of stools at the vacant bar and ordered a double Cuba Libre as a little 'hair-of-the-dog.'

The man behind the bar was rail thin and leather tanned with thinning blond hair and a neatly trimmed gray beard. He wore khaki shorts, a ratty Grateful Dead tee-shirt and ancient boat shoes of decaying blue leather. He could have been anywhere between forty and ninety, but his smile appeared to have all the requisite teeth and he had a spring in his step as he danced along the duck-boards. He stroked a ginger tabby cat that was curled up on the counter in front of him.

"Double Cuba Libre coming right up, Princess," he grinned. "You come down here because you heard about old Sport's repu-tation?"

Margo pulled her head back on her neck and looked at the man. "Huh? Who's this Sport, some local reggae musician or something?"

The barman looked down among his bottles. "Been awhile since I played my guitar with the cats in Haight Ashbury," he mumbled. "I should 'a guessed that you'd be too young to remember me.

"Sports the name, I own this little joint," he held his hand out to shake but when Margo extended her own, he grabbed it, pulled it toward him and kissed the back of it. "The locals aren't big drinkers," he told her, "but I make a living here. Mostly from the crew of the ship that bring things to Cidade Sebastian. Did you just arrive on the boat?"

"Yeah," Margo told him, "From San Juan. Do a lot of ships come in here?"

Sport laughed at that. "Only the one old tub, always the same one, twice a week, unless we need something special like gasoline or water. They'll be bringing me some more American lager and Scotch, although they're the ones that mostly buy the stuff from me and drink it." Sport chuckled to himself as he leaned down and rubbed his head against the tabby cat. The cat emitted a loud purr. "Guess I should be preparing for the onslaught of customers this evening."

"Are there that many on the boat?"

Sport laughed some more. "Well, there's Captain Moore if he's feeling thirsty and First Officer Clemmons who is *always* in need of a drink or three. The crew, who get paid the least, will come in and spend the most. Sometimes the deck hands need to call the island taxi just to get them back down the pier to the gangway.

# Friend

"And when the ship pulls away from the shore, my business dies until they return. I might get a local or two who's had a falling out with his wife or someone celebrating a birthday."

"If it's that bad, why do you stay here?" Margo asked with serious eyes, taking a sip of her Cuba Libre. "You mix a pretty good drink, by the way. You could probably get steady work back in America."

At this, Sport's laughter sounded like a small herd of braying donkeys. "That's rich," he told her, "me going back to America. No thanks, I'd rather stay here and starve… But I'm not starving really." He rubbed the tabby's head then pushed the cat aside. "I've got a pretty decent life here. I mean, I'm the only game in town. They don't even have a bar at the hotel. Someone wants alcohol; I'm the only place to go on the entire island."

"What about the super market," Margo asked, "don't they at least sell beer and wine?"

"Supermarket?" Sport spit back at her with wide eyes. "There's no supermarket on Santa Nepenthe. We've got a butcher, a produce stand and a baker. And the baker doesn't do that well 'cause no one can afford fancy breads and cakes, except for a few rich folks that spend the winter months here."

"So is there a restaurant in this town?" Margo inquired. "I'm not much on cooking for myself."

"You're in it, babe," Sport smiled. "I can fry an egg or two in the morning and put together a pretty good hamburger the rest of the day."

"Only hamburgers?" she asked, looking closely at his face.

"Well, I can do some other stuff, but no one around here seems interested. I can prepare a mean prawn curry or some fair Sonoran enchiladas, but what's the point. The locals catch their own fish and cook it over their fires with their home-grown plantains and carrots."

Their conversation was interrupted by the sound of heavy boots on the wooden wharf outside. "Curry," shouted a red-haired man in a khaki uniform with shirt buttons stretched to bursting over a large beer gut.

"Afternoon, Clemmons," Sport smiled, "your usual?"

"Yeah," the man answered, "but use some kinda decent gin, not that island rotgut you always try to pass off on me."

"You wound me, Officer Clemmons," Sport threw back with a solemn face and a wink at Margo that said we always do this little dance. "The only gin I serve is what you bring to me from the mainland. Have you been tampering with the bottles to cheat me?"

## Chapter Two

**M**argo thoroughly enjoyed Sport's prawn curry. The company wasn't bad either; Rick Clemmons regaled her with fascinating stories about his days in the merchant marine, before his fondness for drink interfered with responsible placement on larger ships. He was thankful that Captain Stephen Moore was an old and trusted friend who would still hire him. It was never mentioned that the MV Dexter, Captain Moore's vessel, was in such a sorry state of disrepair that no one else wanted the post of First Officer. The Dexter only remained in service because Stephen Moore knew a U S Coast Guard inspector who looked the other way for the gifts Moore offered each year.

The other crewmen that showed up at Sport's bar, two Guatemalans and a Filipino, were quite loud and, by the end of the evening very drunk, but were also entertaining to Margo's naive nature. When dinner dishes had been cleared, Sport brought his old Martin guitar from behind the bar and the crewmen joined him in singing old hits from Credence Clearwater and The Jefferson Airplane. One of the Guatemalans, Jaime, borrowed Sport's guitar for a while and crooned some Central American folk songs until he had trouble keeping his eyes open and focused. A brown tabby found its way into Margo's lap and commenced to purring loudly.

Around eleven, Captain Moore came through the door to remind his men that they had to be back in San Juan before dawn. Guatemalan Jaime and Abang, the Filipino, supported First Office Clemmons between them as they headed for the door. Captain Moore downed a straight shot of Jameson's Irish whiskey then followed his crew up the pier, barking out a marching cadence to which no one paid any mind.

Margo shot Sport a questioning look, but Sport just laughed. "Yeah, that's about how it usually goes."

"But," Margo coughed in a distressed voice, "how can they operate a ship in that condition?"

They manage," Sport chuckled. "They have to. If they don't, I'll never have any liquor to sell."

The tabby turned his head up and gave her a feline smile.

Before locking his doors, Sport rang the local Cidade Sebastian taxi to take Margo to her hotel. He waited with her for over half an hour until the cab, an ancient 1950's flathead Ford sedan, showed up. The driver, an old man of mixed race in a long dressing gown and peaked cap, got out and lifted Margo's bags into the car's boot, all the while blinking sleep from his eyes and scowling dagger at his fare for waking him at such an hour.

The Sovereign Hotel was two steep blocks up the hill from Sport's and overlooked the harbor. The cabbie demanded five American dollars for the short ride and gave Margo a dirty look when no tip was offered over and above the tariff. He left her to carry her own bags into the hotel saying, "Next time don't leave it so late," over his departing shoulder.

The lobby of the Sovereign was deserted but for a handful of stray cats with only one dim nightlight burning. "Hello?" Margo shouted, "Anybody home?" When she received no reply, she stepped behind the narrow front desk and picked a key off the board on the wall. Her reservation said she was to have room seven, so that was the key she chose.

Room Seven was on the second floor at the head of the stairs and she couldn't locate an elevator. At least the bed was made in Room Seven, with the top sheet turned back for her and a small French mint resting on her pillow. The bathroom, she noted, had a pile of fluffy white towels, toilet paper and a clean appearing glass by the small sink.

A listing of phone numbers for the island took up less than half a page on top of the bureau and the Gideon bible was in some foreign language, Portuguese, she assumed. Margo started to unpack, searching for her nightgown, but woke up in the clothes she'd arrived in with bright tropical sunlight streaming through the room's large window. Margo got up and went to the window to open the curtains. It was then that she discovered the portal had no glass pane, only a rusting screen to keep the bugs out. "Welcome to paradise," she sighed to herself.

## Chapter Three

Welcome to paradise indeed. Margo took a tepid shower under a thin stream of discolored water, dressed in fresh clothes and headed down the stairs. A milk-chocolate hued young girl sat behind the hotel desk. "Welcome to the Sovereign Hotel, Ms. Drelve," she said with a broad, white smile. "May I have your credit card to make a copy for our file?"

"Of course," Margo smiled back, taking her wallet out of her shoulder bag, "Is there coffee here?

The desk clerk brought a jar of an off-brand instant from behind the desk. "If you let the hot water run for a few minutes it is usually warm enough to dissolve the mix," she assured.

"Breakfast?" Margo inquired already pretty sure of the answer.

"That would be available at Sport's bar," the girl answered with her hundred candle power smile that never quit or faded, "Just down at the bottom of the road. I think they open around ten. We don't allow cooking in our rooms."

"And to connect to the Wi-Fi here in the hotel?" Margo continued.

The desk lady's smile broke for just a moment. "I can give you the password," she told Margo, "but it doesn't always work so well. Just type in Souza, that's the name of the ruling family who grant us all free Internet."

As it was a bright and beautiful morning with a light breeze full of bird song, Margo decided to walk down the steep road to the wharf and Sport's bar. The army of stray cats was camped out by the warehouse door. While she waited for the aging hippie barman to show up, Margo walked south from the wharf area where she discovered a narrow strip of sugar-white sand stretching along the base of steep dark cliffs. She removed her sandals and walked along the water's edge until the sand ended in an outcropping of volcanic rock that blocked further exploration. Margo retraced her steps toward town and when she arrived back by the pier, Sport was just propping his large wooden doors back against the old stone warehouse walls. The small army of stray cats waited for Sport outside the ancient building as if they too were hungry for breakfast.

"Morning princess," he called to her, "Require some 'hair-of-the-dog' or just a little something solid to break your fast?"

Margo had to laugh as she rushed up to the doors of the saloon. "Eggs would be nice. Do you have any potatoes or cheese to mix in with them?"

"That and more," Sport told her. "One of the natives brought me some home grown asparagus and mushrooms to settle his tab. I can whip up an omelet with his offerings that will keep you going all day long, as soon as I put out something for the neighborhood felines."

Margo rolled her eyes at him. "An omelet sounds positively lovely."

Sport disappeared into the back for a short time and returned with two steaming plates. He set them on the bar then proceeded out the front door with a paper plate full of fish heads and other scraps.

"Got to look out for my children," he called over his shoulder.

The omelets were enormous with wide cut British-style 'chips' on the side. He ducked back into the kitchen again and returned with tall glasses of a dirty green colored liquid.

"My own V-8 juice," he told Margo. "I use everything Campbell's claims to put in their canned juice, but I put the fresh vegetables through my own juicer. Vegetables right out of my own garden up on the roof. It's really good for you."

"How about coffee?" Margo asked. "I really need some Mocha Java to get my head started in the morning. All the hotel had to offer was really bad instant."

Sport laughed again. "They've got an old Italian espresso machine there in the office, but they don't like to share it. I have an even better brewing machine. Do you like strong coffee?"

Margo gave Sport a baffled look. "I suppose so," she told him, "I mean I just need a strong caffeine jolt to start my day."

Almost before she finished speaking Sport had a steaming miniature ceramic cup and saucer on the bar in front of her. "Our local beans are better than that Blue Mountain strain in Jamaica. We just don't export them, except on a very limited basis, like through the winter folks that have homes here, but they only send them off to their special friends. We don't sell anything commercially."

"But, if this coffee is so good, why not promote it and let the world know?"

"Not what the Souza family wants," Sport chuckled. "We all just want to protect our island from the crazy commercial world out there."

"So tell me about this Souza clan," Margo asked forking the last of her omelet into her face.

"Well," Sport began with a faraway look in his eyes, "From what I've learned here, the Portuguese made the first claim on this island in the late 1600s. Later, in 1782, the British arrived to run the Portuguese out. Being brilliant imperialists, however," Sport winked at her, "the Brits decided to keep the ruling dynasty, the Souza family, as governors of the island. For some two-hundred-forty years there's always been a Souza ruling the island as though it were some kind of medieval fiefdom."

"Wow!" Margo exclaimed, "And they're still in power?"

"Yeah, but just barely," Sport told her. "The current ruler, Emmanuel Souza, hasn't produced a son to take the reins of power. The man has a highly qualified *daughter* who is more than up to the job."

"So the daughter will become the new ruler?" Margo asked.

"Not as easy as all that," Sport told her. "Santa Nepenthe has always had a male **Supreme Leader**. We have a strongly male oriented society on the island."

As Margo listened, the tabby cat from the previous evening leapt into her lap and rubbed his head against her arm.

"When efforts to product a male heir were failing, Emmanuel sent his oldest girl child, Amelia, to the University of California at Berkeley for advanced degrees in Economics and Political Science, but he was still unsure if this would impress his island subjects. It didn't, and in the past few months there has been talk of an election. The people of Santa Nepenthe want to be given the choice between the daughter of pure Souza blood and someone else, anyone else. There's even been talk of electing one of the very knowledgeable off-islanders who have winter homes here.

"The top off-islander candidate in the race is a real goof-ball named Alphonse Friend, a man full of pipe dreams who talks of all kinds of castles in the air. He claims to be a successful business man in the United States where he owns hotels, casinos and golf courses. While the Souza family stresses unity as a nation living to Christian-Catholic family values, Friend makes big promises about bringing tourists and their money to Santa Nepenthe. Friend's promises hold a certain appeal to the locals who have only recently been introduction to the Internet and its display of worldly opulence. Sites like EBay, Amazon and Facebook have created a strong appetite for things to consume."

Margo stared at Sport wide-eyed. "But this is an unspoiled paradise. Who could ask for anything more?"

"The crushed rock roads on Santa Nepenthe," Sport continued, are barely stable enough for donkey traffic. The only motor cars here belong to the royal family, a few of their neighbors and the small taxi cab company, but now everyone wants a car, preferably a big muscle car like a Camaro or Mustang."

"My God," Margo gasped. "Is this true. Don't they know?" Her outburst startled the tabby in her lap who gave a hiss in protest and leapt onto the bar.

"Margo, Baby," Sport purred, "you and I, we've seen all this big city shit; traffic jams, smog alerts, drive-by shootings... But these poor innocents don't have any experience with these things. The Internet only shows them Michael Jackson dancing and the Home Shopping Channel selling discounted merchandise, trinkets to which they've never had access before."

As Sport's words hung in the air, a pale white man in an even whiter chauffer's uniform and military style cap walked through the oaken double doors from the wharf. He approached the bar with a gallon sized brown glass container in his hand, what's known as a 'growler,' a bottle to transport home brewed beer.

"I need another fill-up for Mr. Friend," the man announced.

"Regular or high test," Sport asked the man with a broad grin.

"Mr. Friend doesn't drink *light* beer," the chauffer scoffed. "Make it something strong and full-bodied."

Sport winked at Margo as he held the bottle under the Budweiser tap. Anyone who sent a growler for weak beer he could buy in a commercial can had to be totally clueless.

As the man walked out with his growler, Margo and Sport broke out in loud laughter. "This guy thinks Budweiser is strong and full bodied?" Margo guffawed. "What kinda klutz is this?"

"The guys who wants to run against Amelia Souza for **Supreme Leader**," Sport laughed. "Now do you understand a little about this place?"

"Not my problem," Margo chuckled. "I'm just here to write my great American novel and go back to my job with the New York Tribune."

# Friend

"So you don't care about our local politics?" Sport asked with a questioning face.

"I'll be long gone before any of this can be a problem," Margo said, tossing back her shoulder length dark hair. "Maybe you should consider returning to California if it's such a big thing."

## Chapter Four

After breakfast, Margo returned to the Sovereign Hotel, fetched her laptop from her room and took it out onto the red-tiled veranda overlooking the Caribbean. She found the link for island Internet, clicked it and waited… and waited. At last a page loaded asking for her password. Margo typed in **souza** as advertised in the hotel's brochure and two cartoon dolphins swam in a circle chasing each other's tails. After some five minutes, a page came up welcoming her to the Santa Nepenthe free community web.

Margo put in the address for her email account. The dolphins returned to circle for another three minutes before an error message appeared telling her there was no Internet service at this time. She tried again and again for over an hour without any progress.

Finally, Margo packed up her computer and carried it down the hill to Sport's place. It was getting on for lunch time anyway.

"Do you have a plug I can use?" she asked the barman. "I can't seem to get a signal up at the hotel and my battery is almost dead. And I could really use a beer as well."

Sport brought a heavy-duty orange outdoor garden extension cord from behind the bar. "I'm not surprised," he chuckled. "We have free Wi-Fi, but that isn't saying much. Do you see that pole sticking out of the water there near the pier?"

Margo turned her head, squinted a bit and made out a silver metal stick about thirty feet tall rising from the surf just off the rocks. "Yeah, I think so," she said.

"That's our Wi-Fi tower," Sport told her. "It's great at sea level, on *this* side of the island, but it doesn't go much farther. Most of the locals pay the Souza family for the cable that connects to it. I don't think the hotel subscribes."

"So the free Wi-Fi?"

"Is a great selling point," he said, setting a frosty mug next to Margo's laptop. "But it's pretty worthless really.

"The islanders, however, will pay anything to get their connection to the outside world."

As Sport finished speaking, Margo's computer had rebooted and was again asking for a Wi-Fi password. This time, the connection came right up and quickly connected to Margo's email. And the tabby cat was also there on the bar staring into her eyes.

She was silent and oblivious to Sport and the stray as she read the dozens of messages that had piled up since she had left New York. Sport stood by, knowing better than to interrupt.

When Margo looked up from her screen, Sport asked if she might be hungry again.

"French fries," Margo breathed, eyes still focused on her computer. "Or onion rings... Can I get both? With lots of ketchup?"

Sport laughed loudly. "Nothing more substantial? No fish or a hamburger sandwich?"

"I've got some serious writing to do," Margo breathed heavily. "I need finger food, carbs… and more beer. I think the thread of my novel is coming to me."

Sport kept Margo supplied with French fries, rings and beer as she ran rapid digits over the keyboard of her laptop, the strange cat fast asleep in her lap. A pair of locals came in, had a beer and went back to their jobs. A very dark complicated man in a dog's collar style shirt stopped by to rail about the sinfulness of drink, and a handful of teen-age girls approached the bar looking for some stimulation.

Sport offered the young girls glasses of weak Shandy, lager with lemonade, and told the man of God not to knock it if he hadn't tried it. Of course, Sport knew that this local reverend had tried it many times as he, Sport, had been the one calling the taxi to take him home to his parish house on the other side of the island.

Just as the priest's taxi was pulling away, there was a rumble of thunder that scattered the stray cats from Sport's front doorway. Within minutes, the island afternoon was dark as night and heavy rains pounded the boards of the wharf. Margo turned on her stool and watched in amazement as the water slammed down like pellets of lead.

"And that's our water supply," Sport told her over her shoulder, "Looks like we'll have enough drinking water for the next twenty-four hours."

Margo rotated her stool back to the man with a puzzled look. "The rainwater will run off into our many underground cisterns to replenish the island's supply," Sport lectured. "Have you noticed that the roofs of all the big buildings are slanted inward like butterfly wings? Every structure has a wide column of clay pipe to collect the water that lands on the roof as it rolls inward to the center and carries it to tanks in our basements. Up in the hills, we have vast stretches of concrete along the slopes that funnel water into the major cisterns. We're just lucky that it rains almost every afternoon... usually right around three o'clock. You could almost set your watch by it."

Within twenty minutes, just as suddenly as it had started, the downpour ceased. Margo swiveled back to check it out and saw dozens of cats spilling forth from their sheltered places to lap up the puddles that had formed.

By late afternoon, Margo's computer told her that she had written some six-thousand words. She scrolled back to the top of the file and began to review her work, after which she screamed, "God, no." The cat quickly disappeared from her lap.

Sport put another beer in front of her. "This one's on the house," he told her with a serious face. "So is something wrong?"

"It's garbage. Everything I've written is garbage. I don't have a clue what I'm doing here. I'm trying to write a mystery and the characters, so far, are all wrong. The setting sucks and I'm about to have a major meltdown."

Sport turned Margo's laptop around facing himself. "Let me see what you've got here," he told her.

Margo drank beer too fast as Sport poured over her screen. When he finally looked up, he told her, "You certainly got my attention. I think you've got something here. Don't be so hard on yourself. Just keep following your thread and I think you'll do fine.

You've got a great style as a storyteller, and I'm not just saying that."

Margo stared at Sport, slightly drunk and very dumbfounded. "You think so," she murmured softly.

"Hey girl," he chuckled, "I'm the audience here. I'm typical of the kinda guy who would buy a book like this, trust me."

Margo smiled and hiccoughed, then shoved another ketchup coated fry into her mouth. "The premise is okay?" The cat appeared from down the counter, snatched a French fry and dragged it to the floor.

"It's great," Sport told her. "You can further develop the characters later when you decide where the plot is going."

Margo climbed carefully off her barstool, walked around the bar to give Sport a big hug, nearly collapsing once or twice on the short journey.

By now dusk was falling across the harbor. Margo had put in a full day of creating and it wasn't clear just how she might be able to negotiate the hotel stairway even if the island taxi brought her up the hill.

Sport could see this and being a gentleman, he offered her his bed above the bar. "I can sleep on the couch," he told her, "I've done it more times than I can count."

Margo just gave him big moony eyes as he put an arm around her and helped her up the stairs. True to his word, Sport helped Margo under the thin sheet on his bed and took himself out to his living room.

## ☀ Chapter Five ☀

argo awoke to confusion. She was in a strange, narrow bed with a tabby cat on her chest within something like a tent of colorful tie-died panels. There was a picture of Che Guevara on one wall and Jimi Hendrix on the opposite. She could hear loud snoring from beyond the room's closed door. Margo badly needed to find a bathroom. She threw back the sheet that covered her to find that she was fully clothed in the apparel she'd worn the previous day.

Margo brushed the cat away, swung her legs over and placed her unsteady feet on the floor. After a couple of attempts, she was able to stand and took some explorative steps. There was a door near the head of the bed leading to a cramped bathroom, no more than three-feet square including a dripping, rusting shower.

Margo sat and peed for a full two minutes, then splashed cold water on her face and ran fingers through her tangled dark hair. "Where the fuck am I?" she mumbled. The cat answered her, but she didn't have a clue what he was saying.

When she exited back into the hippie looking bedroom, she noticed that the snoring had stopped. "Are you decent?" a voice called from the door.

"No," she answered. "I'm a liberal journalist, and relentless at that."

The door at the other end of the room opened, the tabby ran out and Sport's laughter filled the portal. He stood there with a big grin staring at her. "So, will this be another chapter in that amazing mystery you're writing?"

Margo was at a total loss for words. "This is your place?" she inquired. "I never got back to my hotel?"

Sport chuckled. "You're safe here, princess. I'm a fan. I'd like to be in your story but I'm not about to force myself into your life. Besides, I kinda enjoy your company. You're probably the most interesting person that's landed on these shores in the time I've been here."

Margo took hesitant steps across the room to where Sport stood. She threw her arms around him, hugged him tightly and in a hoarse voice asked, "So what's for breakfast?"

The old blue neon clock behind the bar told Margo that it was just coming up to ten. Sport was busy behind the bar feeding fresh basil, kale, cucumber, celery and carrots into a loudly raucous old juicing machine. When the machine stopped, Sport turned with two tall glasses of his home made V-8 juice.

"I'm having a little hair of the dog in mine," he told her bringing a bottle of Estonian vodka from under the counter and holding it up to her, "How about you?"

"Whatever," Margo replied, feeling a threatening pulse across her forehead.

Sport poured a generous shot of alcohol into each glass, stirring them with the knife he'd used to cut the vegetables, and then set one before her on the bar.

"Now for the omelets?" he questioned, "How about spinach, tomatoes and feta cheese?"

# Friend

Margo took a swallow of the murky juice and thought for a minute. She was feeling a bit queasy at first, but when the veggie juice hit her system she make a quick recovery. "Lovely," she replied with a small smile.

Sport busied himself while Margo tried to piece the previous day together in her mind. She fired up her laptop, which was still open on the bar, and checked what she'd written the day before. She smiled with pleasure at the first few chapters then noticed that her grammar and sentence structure seemed to deteriorate as the story went along. How many beers had she consumed throughout the day? And at what point did her writing start to slide?

Oh well, if she went over it all carefully, she could probably save a lot of what she'd attempted to write; the basic plot ideas all seemed to be sound. And Sport had said that he enjoyed her story so far. She was about to begin revisions when the old hippie slid a huge plate of potatoes and eggs in front of her.

"Fortification for a tough day of creating," he told her, setting a knife and fork next to her plate. "I'm not expecting much business again today, so you'll have some peace and quiet for your writing. Do you want to stay at the bar or would you prefer a quiet table in the back corner?"

"But you hardly had any other customers yesterday," she stated with a worried look. "How can you afford to stay in business?"

"I manage," Sport said with a wink. "The supply ship will be back day after tomorrow and I'll sell a substantial amount of food and drink when they land."

"I can't say that I understand business," Margo said with a worried look, "but two semi-busy days in a dead week? How do you survive on that?"

Sport laughed again. "I send meals and beer up the hill to the Souza family every day. They never question their bill and, believe me, they pay four times what customers at the bar give me. And they always tip twenty-percent or more, same thing with this Friend guy and a few of the winter folks when they're on the island. I've had this place for just over fifteen years next month. Don't worry about this old hippie peace freak. I do okay for myself."

Margo pushed her computer aside and gave Sport a serious look. "How did you end up in this place, anyway? I mean why would you choose a place like this?"

"Well," Sport answered with a sheepish look, stroking another stray cat that crossed the bar, "I didn't actually *choose* Santa Nepenthe. You might say it chose *me*. Or maybe the Gods just thought I should be here..."

"Oh come on," Margo chuckled. "Gods thought you should open a bar on a rock with no fresh water and an old dictator?"

"Souza's not exactly a dictator," Sport defended. "He honestly loves all his people and tries to do what's best for them."

"It still sounds like he's a dictator to me," Margo scolded, "but settings that aside, how did you happen to land here?"

It was Sport's turn to laugh. "You really want to know?"

"Hey, I asked, didn't I?"

"Well," the old hippie drawled. "I was being chased by the Coast Guard, like the US Coast Guard." With this statement, the man's eyes almost closed and he dug fingers into the cat's back as he remembered the details of his long ago story.

"And, pray tell, why would the US Coast Guard be chasing you way out in the Caribbean?" she asked, closing her laptop and folding her hands on the bar.

"Three of the Virgin Islands are owned by America, so the US patrols the water around them; St. Thomas, St. Johns and St. Croix. The Coast Guard does search and rescue here along with… well, ah, looking for smugglers, I guess you'd say."

"Don't tell me, you were smuggling something?" Margo inquired with a half grin, elbows on the bar and her chin resting on the backs of her hands.

"Just a little marijuana from Jamaica," Sport replied, nodding his head. "It was no big deal."

"Just how much pot did you have that was 'no big deal'?" Margo said, her face turning serious.

"Ah, five hundred pounds," Sport squeaked with a lopsided grin.

"Five hundred pounds of pot?" Margo barked, lifting her head from her hands. "Where were you taking this load of drugs?"

"Not drugs, just a little ganja," the old hippie corrected in a soft, timid voice as he ran his fingers along the cat's chin. "I had a buyer waiting on the west coast of Florida."

"Florida's a long way from the Virgin Islands," Margo pointed out.

Sport was silent for a moment. He raised his hands to his head and massaged his temples before speaking again. "I never got to Florida," he said, his voice still *sotto voce*. "We were sailing an old shrimp boat registered in Texas. I guess it looked out of place cruising past Charlotte Amalie harbor, so a patrol boat came out to board us. My friend panicked, gave the old tub full throttle and we tried to outrun them. We had almost lost the 65-foot cutter when we ran over a shallow reef and tore a hole in the rotting wood hull of the shrimper. Jared, my captain and buddy, just kept leaning on the throttles but as we kept running, water was rapidly pouring into our bilges."

"And your boat and all your drugs sunk to the bottom." Margo tsked.

"Not exactly," Sport told her. "We *almost* outran them in spite of the blown hull. I was on the foredeck guiding us, but I didn't see that there was another shallow reef in our path. We hit the coral, which threw me forward over the bow. I hit the water, dove deep and kept swimming as fast as I could. When I surfaced, some 300 yards to the left, I saw the Coast Guardsmen storming our old boat. They arrested Jared and started packing up our ganja as evidence. I ducked under the water again and swam with all my might for the only island I could view on the horizon."

"Santa Nepenthe," Margo guessed.

"Well, yeah," Sport replied. "At first I wasn't sure of what I was getting myself into. I washed up on the beach just east of Cidade Sebastian where I was rescued by a pair of young ladies who brought me fresh water and mangoes. They helped me up the hill to see their older brothers. The relatives all liked to smoke a little dope and couldn't see why the US was so against it as to be pursuing me."

"Lucky for you." Margo interjected. "And the Coast Guard hadn't followed?"

"I learned from my new friends that Santa Nepenthe was never formally recognized by the United States, so they had no extradition treaties. At least for the time, I was safe on these rocky shores."

Margo laughed loudly. "Lucky for you, but somehow you acquired a bar and restaurant here?"

"Just let me tell the story," Sport went on. "There was an old stone pirate warehouse on the dock in Cidade Sebastian, this warehouse we're sitting in. At one time it held a booty of gold, silver and other treasures, but with the decline of piracy it became less and less important. For a short while, local growers hung tobacco and marijuana plants here for curing. During American prohibition, liquor smugglers kept supplies of Scotch in the warehouse awaiting shipment to Texas and Florida, but with the repeal of prohibition the place sat vacant for a few decades.

"When I suddenly turned up on the beach, an emissary of the Souza family approached me about opening a bar and restaurant in the space."

"How did they know you could cook or tend bar?" Margo asked.

"They didn't," Sport told her, now stroking the feline's tummy. "But they made it clear that if I could start cooking for the family and serving alcohol to the natives that were interested in taking a drink they wouldn't send me back to America and they would give me this old derelict warehouse free of charge. If not, they'd use me to win some political mileage. What could I do?"

Margo grinned. "So you became the only game in town for food and drink."

Sport hung his head. "You might say that, but it hasn't been a bad life, better than Jared has had all these years in a Florida prison."

"You know your friend is in prison?"

"I get letters from Jared from time to time, sent through a network of old friends. He told me at first that the guys in Florida that financed our venture weren't at all happy. They put out a contract on my life, another reason that I can't go back to the US. My life would be worth about the price of a bottle of RC Cola if I was back home in California."

## Chapter Six

"**B**ut don't you miss America? Don't you sometimes wish you could go home?"

"Not a chance." Sport smiled at Margo. "It was already getting too weird the last time I was there."

"So then why were you running so much marijuana if you didn't want to cop the American Dream?" Margo asked, her face serious and questioning.

"Well," Sport began, "I could have used a little nest egg to start a new life somewhere in Europe or in the islands… but mainly I had a huge debt to pay off in student loans. I didn't want that dogging me around. And, I thought the US pot laws were totally unfair. It was a kinda protest act. Can you understand that?"

Margo laughed. "You tried to shoot yourself in the foot as a protest."

Sport looked down at his feet behind the bar. "I wouldn't want to look at it like that, but in hindsight I guess you might have something there."

Margo laughed louder, "You poor, silly man." Then with a more somber face, she confided, "I might have done the same thing back in my college days. I was quite an activist back then."

"Yeah, well those were certainly different times," Sport replied, his shoulders drooping and some of the light going out of his eyes. "I used to believe in a lot of that…" The cat on the bar made sympathetic chattering noises.

Margo reached over the bar and took his hand. "And you've lost all that? You don't have any faith left in humanity? I used to write stories for the Trib every day about the bad things people do to one another, but I still have faith that we're not all bad. We can't let the few negative beings out there pull all the good ones down."

Sport gave a hollow laugh. "I guess I'm happy for you," he said. "Me, I'll just hide out here in my quiet little corner and wait for the end. I'm sorry, but for all I've seen, I can't, or maybe I won't, expect too much of the free world or the human race. These stray cats along the waterfront are the only living beings I really trust."

She didn't know why, but Margo leaned across the bar and gave Sport a kiss. "It really isn't all that bad," she told him. "You just have to believe in things."

"I believe I'll have another drink," Sport said with a wink, pulling the Estonian vodka bottle from under the bar. "You want a snort?" he asked.

Margo took the proffered shot glass but turned away from the hippie bar man. She drew her laptop closer to her, flipped the cover up and clicked the icon to reopen her word file. Somehow, she told herself, this should all be a part of my novel. But her novel was a mystery, set in another time and place. Was there a way to bring the two together? The tabby tried to stretch out on her keyboard.

Margo pushed the puss aside and read over her manuscript from the time she'd landed on Santa Nepenthe. Her story was all about a rogue policeman in New York City, but in review it was too much like a hundred other New York stories. She'd been reading too many novels by Lawrence Sanders, Ed McBain and Lawrence

Block. It was all garbage. It didn't matter what Sport told her. She had to begin all over again.

Margo vowed to pay the Internet connection fee from the local government to get a clear connection at her hotel. It was madness trying to write in a waterfront bar where she spent her days drinking ale and vodka.

On the other hand, she would still have to visit Sport's bar at least twice a day to take her meals. The hotel didn't even have a microwave that she could use to heat things. Margo still couldn't believe that an island of some fifteen-hundred-plus people didn't have a supermarket or even a small neighborhood grocery store.

Margo resolved to call a taxi the next morning and ask the driver to take her all around Santa Nepenthe so that she might see for herself that there was no marketplace or town center where food could be bought.

The next day's island tour proved a true disappointment. There was, indeed, nothing like a brick-and-mortar market. There was very little of anything outside of Cidade Sebastian, not even a 'four-corners' where people congregated. Along her drive they didn't encounter as much as a gas station, but then she should have guessed this as there were only three or four cars on the island.

A few of the locals had signs outside their huts advertising mangoes and papayas for sale or 'handy man will work cheap.' And at every turn in the road, Margo saw more of those patches of concrete or asphalt along the hillsides that could catch rainwater and collect it beneath the earth's surface. One canyon they drove along actually had what looked like an old Roman aqueduct connecting the slopes on either side to bring water down to the city.

The cabbie stopped before a large stone structure with statues in niches along the walls and twelve foot high oak doors. He held the car door open and motioned her out of the old Ford, then bowed and crossed himself as he turned to the structure.

"This is the Cathedral of Santa Nepenthe." He announced, "The most holy site on our island."

"Cathedral?" Margo squeaked.

"You must cover your head with a hat or scarf," the taxi man told her. "Then I may give you a tour of this sacred place and introduce you to Father Roboza." They walked up the steps, careful not to step on the many assembled stray cats in front of the granite building.

Margo wasn't even a Christian, much less a Catholic, but she dug a faded handkerchief out of her handbag and laid it over her head as she followed the cabbie into the cavernous structure.

Father Roboza was the same man that had been in Sport's the day before railing against strong drink. The cab driver, who Father Roboza addressed as Senhor Morais, dropped to one knee near the altar, spoke rapid Portuguese and lit a number of candles before standing up. "Please, senhora, can I not say prayers for someone close to you?"

Margo was totally lost. She stared blankly at the man, finally asking, "Could we just get on with the tour?"

From that point, the taxi man had little to say to her. He woodenly pointed out highlights, like the sugar-sand beach on the island's north side, the mill where cane was turned into sugar and the Souza Palace on the highest point of the rock where the government was centered for the island. The rains came as they crossed the island heading back to the city, falling so hard the wipers on the old Ford taxi couldn't keep up. The taxi man had to pull over for a few minutes. They sat in silence until the downpour subsided. Margo and the cab driver were both relieved when the man dropped her back at the hotel in Cidade Sebastian.

"What kind of lame was I to choose such a place," Margo asked herself when the taxi man held the door for her that evening. But, of course, a girl who'd grown up in Minneapolis and spent her adult life in the big apple wasn't expected to know that much about primitive Caribbean islands.

By nightfall, Margo found herself walking back down the grade to the waterfront where she parked herself on a stool at Sport's place and ordered a Prawn Vindaloo for supper along with a large ale. The tabby cat that had chosen her was there waiting by her place at the bar.

"Good to see you," Sport grinned. "I was wondering where you were."

"I asked the taxi driver to give me the nickel tour of the island," Margo smiled. "It wasn't long before I started wondering why either one of us is here. I mean when I was looking at places to go to write, I never even considered that there might be countries that didn't have a supermarket or a restaurant."

"I've got a restaurant here," Sport interjected.

"And, when I found the website for the hotel here, I just assumed the place would have a coffee shop and room service. What a naive fool I've been."

"Didn't old Morais point out that the bakery is just two doors up the hill from the hotel? You can get something to eat there if you get tired of my cooking. Also, the butcher, just behind the hotel, sometimes sells whole fried chickens."

With this, Sport laughed. "Welcome to the third world. I'm sure this isn't the only backward island in these waters. But I'm happy that you chose this one. I'm thoroughly enjoying your company here."

Margo raised her glass of beer in a toast. "That makes two of us," she giggled. "I think talking with you may give me a whole new slant on the book I'm writing. By the way, does this cat that seems to have adopted me have a name?"

"That's Einstein," Sport laughed. "He's got his own theory of relativity… If he likes you, you're an instant relative."

## ☀ Chapter Seven ☀

Margo slept late the next morning, feeling a little depressed about her situation. But when she threw back the curtains in her room, her ears were greeted by the sound of birdsong, and the bright tropical sunshine flooded her room. She wished she had strong coffee right there to get her started, but then thought about Sport's place waiting just down the hill.

The first thing I'm going to do today when I fire up my computer, she told herself, will be to order an espresso machine and a small bean grinder on line and have it sent to the hotel. Sport can get me a local supplier for Santa Nepenthe coffee beans. Life will instantly get better when I have coffee at my beck and call. That plus a reliable Internet connection right here in my hotel room. Maybe I can even have a microwave shipped in.

"A microwave?" Sport questioned when Margo was seated at the bar waiting for her breakfast, Einstein the tabby sitting patiently near her place on the counter. "Do you have some secret source for frozen TV dinners or something?"

"Well, I'm thinking I could at least boil rice or cook fish. There *is* someplace to buy fresh caught fish or rice on the island, isn't there?"

Sport brayed his own special laughter at her. "Sure, there're a few locals that will sell some fish when they've caught more than they can eat but we don't grow rice here, the climate is too dry. The stuff I get is shipped in once a month, and I pay a premium for it… But I'll be glad to share some with you.

"You can't even get microwave popcorn on this rock. That's how backward this place is. If you want to boil rice and fry fish you'd be better off to invest in a hotplate. And I know a guy that sells those cheap right here in Cidade Sebastian."

Margo raised her face in a sheepish grin. "So what else am I missing here? Is there someplace where the farmers sell what they can't eat? I mean besides the odd yard sale out in the boonies?""

"Saturday mornings," Sport replied with a wink, "we have a sort of farmer's market right out on the dock. What day is today anyway? I tend to lose track unless we have a supply ship coming in, is this Saturday? They might just be setting up out there right now. They sell local bananas, pineapple, mangoes, coconuts and peppers. Sometimes they even have lettuce and cabbage depending on who's selling."

"How come the cab driver didn't mention this?" Margo inquired.

Sport gave another chuckle. "You're an American tourist," he explained. "The locals expect you to have servants that take care of such things. They believe that all American tourists are rich. Why would you soil your hands with such common things as shopping or cooking?"

"I didn't think you got that many tourists here," Margo said with an astonished look.

"Oh, we have a few regulars," he nodded. "There's a condo complex on the eastern coast. Didn't the cabbie show this development to you?"

# Friend

"I don't recall that we even drove along the east coast. He was very anxious to show me the cathedral, and the Souza residence at the top of the island. Other than that it was just lovely beaches and not-so-lovely villages of grass shacks."

"Typical," Sport chuckled. "He's probably paid plenty to protect the privacy of the foreigners that can afford to live here in style. The Souza family allowed outside interests to build the complex, it's called Vista Para o Mar, Portuguese for 'view of the sea'. These rich folks own their places but the land underneath them is on a fifty year lease from the Souza family, so what do they actually own? It will eventually all go back to the Souza kids in the next generation. That is if the rich bastards don't trash the place first."

"So cynical," Margo burst out. "Just because they're rich, they won't respect someone else's property?"

"More a case of 'if I can't have it forever, no one else will either' is what I think," Sport shot her a stone face. "Hey, I send food and drink out to these people. I think I can give a fair judgment of what kind of folks they are."

Margo ate her poached eggs on crab cakes in silence, thinking about Sport's assessment of the island's people. When she'd finished her eggs, which she ended up sharing with Einstein, and two cups of strong coffee, she motioned the barman back to her place at the counter.

"The first thing I need to do," she told Sport, "is to secure an Internet connection for my hotel room. Who do I contact to get myself connected?"

Sport thought for a minute. "That would probably be Junior Souza, the Supreme Leader's nephew. He handles most of the island's inland business. You want me to ring him up?"

"That would be swell," Margo crooned.

Junior Souza was at the bar in less than twenty minutes with contract forms printed in triplicate for Margo to sign. The man wanted payment in US cash dollars, but eventually agreed to put the toll on a Visa card for a 2% surcharge. Junior left the bar after three beers, assuring Margo that she would have Internet on island Wi-Fi at her hotel by the next dawn.

When Junior Souza left, Margo strolled out onto the dock just in time to catch the final hour of the produce market. She purchased local fruit that she could snack on as well as some salad greens for when she didn't feel like venturing down the hill to Sport's place. She even found an elderly lady that had loaves of course dark bread and cakes. She bought some *pão doce* that would go with coffee when she didn't feel like venturing out too early.

Back at Sport's, Margo didn't even bother to open her laptop. She ordered a double gin martini and stared out through the wide double doors at the harbor where the marketplace people were packing up their wares.

"Everyone here is anxious to collect American dollars," She mused. "What is the local currency, anyway? I mean they *do* have a local currency, don't they?"

Sport gave his typical burst of loud laughter. "It's called the Gourd," he chuckled, "you know, like a dried hollow squash thing?"

"The Gourd?" Margo asked with a surprised look. "The Gourd? Like on the flag? What does that mean?"

"Well," Sport began with a grin, "as I learned in my time here, since there's no source of natural water on Santa Nepenthe, people had to collect water from puddles and barrels. They stored it in gourds, like the huge seed-pods of certain plants. Any man with many gourds of water was considered wealthy. He could survive a drought while his neighbors perished from thirst. What could be more valuable than water or the vessels that saved it? Gourds saved water, something more valuable to survival than gold. Hence, the Gourd."

"Oh that must be some kind of fable," Margo giggled.

"No, it is the God's truth," came a voice from the doorway. Junior Souza stood there back-lighted by the setting sun. "I came to bring you your credit card receipt and overheard your conversation. It is true that in the days of my great, great grand uncle there was a time when no rain fell for many months. Those with many gourds filled with water could name their price for almost anything. My family stayed in power only because we had placed a large reservoir on the roof of our palace. Our water became stale and bad tasting before the drought passed, but we were able to boil this bad water and stay alive. Many of the peasants perished from drinking foul water. Those who kept their gourds in cool caves also survived and as a result, the Gourd became our national currency."

## Chapter Eight

When Junior had departed back to the Souza compound, Margo gave Sport a strange look. "This guy is a specimen of the people in charge?" she asked. "He reminds me of some of the pizza delivery guys I've met in Brooklyn."

"Only, we don't have pizza delivery service here on Santa Nepenthe," Sport chuckled, "So he collects money for his uncle, the Supreme Leader. I think it all makes some weird kind of sense."

"Ever thought of starting a pizza franchise here?" Margo asked with a wicked grin. "It might be a big success."

"No thanks," Sport laughed. "I've got too much on my plate as it is. I'm not even sure these hicks know what pizza is."

"Oh, I think they know what it *is*," Margo told him with a thoughtful pose. "They just don't know where to buy it. Try having the supply boat bring in a few hundred cheap frozen pizzas, offer them on the menu, and see what happens."

"I'm not sure I'd even want to know what would happen," Sport told her. "I've got more business right now than I'll ever need. Let's just not mention the word pizza to anyone around here. If you want a pizza, just tell me and I'll try and make one if there's no one around, but I don't want to deal with some new crazy island fad."

Margo threw her head back in a full-throated bray.

"What, what is it?" Sport whispered anxiously.

"It's you." she hollered. "You're such a hypocrite. You're posing as an American bar in this banana republic, but you don't want to expand your menu to reflect any kind of true American menu. You only want to sell what's comfort food for you; hamburgers, hot dogs, fish and chips and fatty fried breakfasts of potatoes and eggs."

"You wound me, lady." Sport replied with a contrite face. "Haven't I cooked some exotic and tasty dishes for your liking? And don't I prepare curry and other exotic dishes for the sailors that bring in our supplies?"

"I suppose you do," she replied. "But does anyone else on the island know what you're capable of preparing? Do you ever send your curry dishes or spicy pastas up to the royal family?"

"The royals up at the palace are a meat-and-potatoes kinda crowd," Sport told her. "They've no taste for variation. I've sent some exotic dishes to the rich folk's condominiums on the east shore, but they're the only ones with open culinary minds. And the best money I make there is bringing in California wines. But they don't consume enough to get me a good mark-up on the stuff."

"So who are these 'east coast' people," Margo asked. "And just how many condominiums are there in that area?"

Sport leaned over the bar close to Margo's ear and whispered, "The commoners aren't suppose to know much about Vista Para o Mar. The only ones in the know are the islanders that act as servants; butlers, maids and room-cleaners. And those folks sign a contract that they won't talk about their positions to any other island residents.

"I've heard that the Souza family built around ninety dwellings on the cliffs over Santa Nepenthe's most beautiful sugar sand beach. They even dredged a yacht harbor nearby. A couple of the Souza children live there beside the wealthy snow-birds that have bought dwellings on the island. It's also rumored that there are a lot of vacancies that the royal family would like to fill."

"And how do they propose to do this?" Margo was truly curious.

"They advertise in a lot of American travel magazines. But, unfortunately Santa Nepenthe doesn't have any real credibility. It's like advertising some kind of mythical Magic Island that you need to travel through time to find. Most of the folks looking for a retirement hide-away want a place vetted by AARP or some large US bank."

"But a number of people *have* bought into this, what did you call it? Vista Para o Mar? Why don't they spread the word to friends or other retirees? It would seem like they would want a bigger community here to share."

"I couldn't answer that," Sport told her. "Maybe they're hiding from something, or just very reclusive. From what I've seen when I've gone up there, they don't advertise bingo games or movie nights. They have a golf course, but you rarely see anyone out on it. Or even out on their perfect white sand beach, for that matter. Heck, it's pretty rare to even see someone sitting on the balconies of the development."

"Are they all septuagenarians or something?" Margo asked with a scrunched-up face. "Too old to be active?"

Sport laughed again. "Hardly," he barked. "Many of them are younger then I am. Maybe they have some kinda secret games and meetings. It's a large complex with quite a few common rooms."

Einstein brushed Margo's shoulder as if to say, "Why would you care about these people when you have me to love?"

Weeks passed as Margo settled on a solid outline for her book. Accompanied by more of the island's stray cats, she did much of her writing on the red-tiled patio of the Sovereign Hotel overlooking the island's docks and using her new, strong Internet connection, while stopping by Sport's place twice daily to take her main meals. When the supply ship was in port, she tended to stay later at the bar, enjoying the stories the crew of the MS Dexter had to tell.

"So how are you enjoying that new German espresso machine?" Captain Moore asked one evening.

"I'm still waiting for it to arrive," Margo told the man. "It seems to be taking a long time and the website keeps telling me they have no way of tracking my package without a post code. I guess Santa Nepenthe doesn't have any post codes."

Both the captain and his first officer turned on their barstools to give her questioning looks.

"What is it?" Margo asked, her eyes shifting between the two of them.

"We delivered your package about three weeks ago," First Officer Clemmons announced. "I walked it up the hill to the front desk myself."

"And you never told *me*?" Margo's voice was shrill and rising in pitch.

"I delivered it, what's to tell?"

"Well, no one has taken the time to tell me that it arrived yet. Are you sure it was my package? And how did you know it was an espresso machine, anyway?"

"Espresso machine was clearly written on the custom's form, along with the brand name and the value of the item," Moore told her. "It had to have this information on the ticket in order to clear the army customs officer on the dock."

Margo became very quiet. "Thank you, gentlemen," she whispered as she pushed her unfinished drink and the accompanying tabby cat aside, climbed down from her stool and exited the bar.

The lady stormed up the hill in a quick march. It was close to midnight when Margo approached the front desk of the Sovereign Hotel. She tapped the old fashioned push-bell on the desk. When there was no response, she banged her fist repeatedly on the small alarm, sending a pair of kittens flying from under the desk. When she still received no satisfaction, she vaulted the low, narrow counter and ran into the office, fists raised and shouting.

The milk-chocolate hued young girl was reclining in a ratty cotton hammock hanging between two of the room's support columns. She sat up, yawned a cavernous yawn and asked, "Is something not to your liking, Ms. Drelve?"

"Damn right something isn't to my liking." Margo screamed. "Where the hell is my espresso machine? I was told that it was delivered here a few weeks ago and no one has said a word to me. So what gives?"

"I know nothing of what you are talking about," the girl replied innocently.

"Package, addressed to me, delivered to this hotel," Margo shouted almost touching noses with the milk-chocolate hued girl.

The girl blinked a few times and replied in a calm, matter-of-fact voice, "Perhaps it arrived when someone else was working the desk."

"Girl. What's your name, anyway? You are *always* behind this desk. I've never seen another soul working around this hotel except the old grandma that cleans my room occasionally."

"I do get a personal day off from time to time," the girl told her with a hurt expression. "And you may address me as Ms. Hix."

"Well, Ms. Hix, I want a word with your boss at the earliest convenience and I want you present at this interview to help me understand where my package has gotten off to, is that understood?"

Ms. Hix gave Margo a smarmy grin. "The owner's are off the island right now. I will let them know of your concern when they arrive home." The girl then lay back in her hammock and pulled a sheet over her face to signify their discussion was finished.

Margo flew up the stairs to her room in a rage, slamming the door behind her so hard it almost popped off its hinges. She lay down and tried to sleep but the whole situation was so upsetting that she tossed and turned, getting up occasionally to pace the floor and shout expletives about the Sovereign Hotel. If there had been any other guests, she most likely would have kept them up all night as well and drawn enough complaints to have her evicted.

Margo finally trudged down the hill to watch the sun rise from the beach near the docks. She kicked off her sandals and waded out into the water, then lay down on the narrow strip of sand where she eventually managed an hour or two of restless sleep. When she awoke, she heard Sport propping open the broad warehouse doors to his establishment. The barman was quiet, sensing Margo's upset state. He went behind the bar without a word, drew a cup of coffee and set it before the distraught woman before he set plates of scraps outside the door for the feral cats.

When Margo had drained her serving of caffeine and had a second cup set before her, she asked, "How do I find the police in this berg."

"We don't actually have police here on Santa Nepenthe," Sport explained with his usual grin.

"No police?" Margo asks, incredulity written all over her face. "What if there's a robbery... or a rape or murder? You must have some kind of police?"

"The army will look into anything like that," Sport chuckled. "Our army takes care of all such breaches of the peace."

"So where do I find this army, then?" Margo asked, neck and shoulders tight under an angry, red face.

"The next warehouse down the dock," Sport told her. "But you don't need to go over there. You'll only find some farmer that's been drafted and assigned desk duty and could care less about your problems... Unless you can offer him a bribe; these conscripts will take anything - from food to a prostitute. American dollars are their favorite."

"So then what am I supposed to do to get my stolen property back?" she practically shouted in the barman's face. "That bitch up at the hotel stole my espresso machine. That's, like tampering with the US Mail.

"First," Sport told her, "Cool it. Get a grip on yourself. Everything will work out just fine... And we don't have US mail here. Once it lands on these shores its *Souza* mail. There's a big difference."

"After I just spent ninety-nine dollars on the Internet for a coffee machine? And another twenty for a bean grinder? I don't think so."

Sport barked out another casual laugh. "So tell me the whole story from the top."

"Sure," Margo replied with downturned eyes. "And you'll lay a bit of sympathy on me. Please."

Sport turned his back to the bar and poured some rum into a glass, adding soda and crushed mint leaves with a dash of sugar. He stirred the concoction and set it on the bar in front of his distraught customer.

"Drink this down and chill for a minute while I tell you a little about the mail here and the Souza government. First, I can get your problem sorted out very quickly."

"I thought I had to check with the army who act as the police?" Margo said after taking a strong pull of her drink. Einstein, the tabby that favored Margo hopped onto the bar then, sensing her anger, jumped down again and headed for the door.

"And that's just what you're doing. On Santa Nepenthe, every able-bodied man is a member of the army reserve. Our regular army is around fifty men, mostly lay-about dudes who can't hold a regular job. The Souza family feeds them, gives them a place to sleep and charges them with keeping the peace.

"The regular army officer corps is all made up from the Souza family and a few wealthy friends, the Supreme Leader being the top general and his brothers, uncles and cousins making up the rest of the elite. Because of my education, the Supreme Leader has commissioned me as a major in the island *reserves*. If we are ever invaded, I'll be expected to lead this common rabble in defense of Santa Nepenthe."

"So, what are you telling me?" Margo inquired.

"I'm saying that, as a major in the Santa Nepenthe army reserves, I can walk up the hill with you and threaten to arrest the hotel staff if they interfere with your mail delivery. Believe me, they'll listen."

"And if they deny taking my things?"

"I will threaten to bring them to judgment before the Souza family."

"What, do they have some kind of Supreme Court or something?"

Sport gave another bray of laughter. "Supreme Court? We have *Papa Souza*, our Supreme Leader, *O Cabeça* he calls himself. He is the island's judge and jury. If he finds someone guilty he can either have them hung or exiled."

"But if they're island natives, where can he exile them to?"

"Ultimately, the sea; exiles are simply given twenty-four hours to leave the island. If they have a boat they can sail away. If they have no boat, they are simply cast off from the cliffs on the western shore to swim for a new life."

Einstein, the tabby, jumped up on the bar and gazed at Margo. "This is all true," he seemed to say.

## Chapter Ten

W
ith a wink, Sport came from behind the counter carrying a sheet of paper that had "Gone shopping" scrawled on it in barely legible magic marker. "It's going to be a slow day anyway," he told her, "no ships due in." The man then taped the placard to the heavy oak door, closed and locked the portal and motioned Margo to follow him to a far corner behind the bar.

Margo treaded lightly into the small private office from which Sport ran the bar's business affairs. The barman opened a claustrophobic closet to one side of the hall and brought forth a white uniform coat with heavy gold braid dripping from the shoulders. He motioned Margo to hold the jacket for him while he slipped his arms into the sleeves, putting on the uniform over his fading Jimmy Buffett for President tee-shirt.

As she was holding the coat for Sport, Margo couldn't help but notice a number of diplomas on the wall above the man's desk. The top sheepskin was from UCLA, naming Patrick Scully Sportacus as a Master of Arts in Political Science.

"Patrick Scully Sportacus?" Margo read out loud.

"Greek father, Irish mother, what can I say?" was the barman's reply. "I was driven to achieve."

Margo's eyes drifted down the wall. There were also diplomas for a BA from Cal State Los Angeles and an Associate degree from Los Angeles City College.

"All these degrees and you end up in a bar in a lesser banana republic?" she asked shaking her head.

"Yeah," Sport laughed. "And I was damn lucky to get this job."

"But so much potential," she lamented. "I'd hire you in a minute as a reporter for my newspaper."

"Thanks," he smiled, "but it wouldn't work out. I just couldn't find anywhere that I fit in… I mean in corporate America. So is my collar straight?"

"Don't you need uniform pants or boots?" Margo asked. "You're going out there in shorts and flip-flops?"

"Well, to call on some petty thief," Sport grinned. "The jacket is threat enough." He reached to a top shelf and retrieved a stiff, white peaked cap with gold braid on the bill and the Santa Nepenthe crest, a seagull standing on a gourd, prominently displayed above the visor.

They walked quickly up the hill together. Entering the Sovereign Hotel, Sport didn't even slow down. He strode through the office door like he owned the place, with Margo in his wake. The milk-chocolate hued girl looked up from her desk in surprise, her gaze going up and down to take in Sport's white dress uniform coat and Margo following close behind.

Ms. Hix stood quickly, dislodging another of the island's ferals from her lap. Before she could say a word in protest, Sport unleashed a barrage of rapid-fire Portuguese that knocked the woman back into her chair. She offered a few weak words of protest, but soon her face collapsed. Margo didn't understand the language, but could sense that the poor girl was mixing a cry of surrender with a plea for mercy.

Sport stood tall over the quivering desk clerk as she melted into her chair. When the bar owner barked a final command, Ms. Hix turned her swivel desk chair to the back wall of her office, stood and opened a large closet. From this storage space she brought forth a cardboard box bearing Amazon logos which she placed before Margo on the front desk counter. A curious ginger kitten leaped up to sniff the box.

Margo was about to say something when the girl turned back to the closet and extracted more parcels. Checking the labels, Margo saw that there was also a digital camera and a photo quality printer addressed to her along with a bean grinder.

"I didn't even remember ordering these," she mumbled to herself. "Wow!"

Sport took two steps forward to the large closet. There were still a number of shipping boxes stacked against the back of the space.

"And these would be?" he asked the girl.

"These folks have already checked out. No forwarding address," the girl spit defiantly at Major Sport.

"Let's take a look," the barman told her, inching closer to the closet door. "Mr. Johan Butterbrot? Didn't he move into the Vista Para o Mar last June? You must have been informed of his new address. And what's this, a patio table for Agnes Frank, who also moved to the royal condos?"

"I was told to hold these things until all their bills were settled," the young girl protested.

"So now, I believe everything is settled, is it not?" Sport declared, eye to eye with the young girl.

"But these people are all *foreigners*," the girl protested. They are not Nepenthen natives. Foreigners, as we know, can't be trusted."

"These are all people who bring money to this island," Sport shouted at the girl. "These people invest in our economy when they buy property on the island and choose to live here. They buy goods from the local farmers and merchants, *and* they pay local taxes to the Souza government."

"I demand an audience with *O Cabeça*," the girl protested.

"And we'll tell him about how you've been collecting people's personal property?" Sport asked. "Do you own a boat? Or do you have friends on some nearby island, within swimming distance?"

"Oh, just go away." the milk-chocolate hued girl whispered angrily, her eyes tearing up. "I won't do anything like this again. I need this job... I thought I was doing what O Cabeça would want me to do. We *must* protect the security of our island."

Sport picked up the phone from Ms. Hix desk and summoned the island's taxi cab, telling Senhor Morais that he had some parcels to be delivered to Vista Para o Mar. "You may send the bill to O Cabeça," he said into the instrument. "Tell him the expense was authorized by Major Sportacus of the Royal Army Reserves." He listened for a moment then replied, "No, I will *not* pay you now and ask our leader to reimburse me. You will do as you are told. Or maybe you'd like to take your taxi over to St Thomas and pay *that* island's taxes?"

# Friend

Sport dropped the phone back into its cradle, shot Margo a wink and executed a very military about face then marched out of the hotel. Margo shrugged her shoulders, smiled at Ms. Hix, and carried all her boxes up to her room before following Sport out and down the hill.

At the bottom of the rise, there was a well dressed man in an ice cream suit and Panama hat pacing in front of the closed warehouse doors.

"Mr. Butterbrot," Sport hailed him. "I've got some good news for you."

"I don't need good news," the portly man replied sourly, "I need a drink, a strong drink."

"Well come on in and name your poison," the bar man smiled, unlocking the large oak doors, pulling loose the crude 'Gone shopping' sign and swinging the doors open. "A double gin martini, dirty?" he winked.

"Shaken, not stirred," the old guy frowned. "Just like that movie spy." The man in white struggled up onto a tall rattan bar stool.

Sport stepped behind the counter, removed his uniform coat which he hung on a hook sprouting from a thick support pillar, and began rummaging around the bottles under the bar. He withdrew an orange colored clay flask labeled Bols and a green bottle of Martini brand dry vermouth, poured some liquid from each into an aluminum shaker, then brought forth a large jar of Spanish olives from the bar fridge. The old hippie poured olive juice into the shaker and clamped the lid on tight, deftly speared two of the large green olives from the jar and tossed them in the air. As the olives fell earthward, he snatched a martini glass from the bar and caught the green fruit in mid air. Setting the glass on the bar top, he grabbed the aluminum shaker, juggled it hand to hand, tossed it skyward behind his back, spun around and caught it to give it a few more serious shakes, then poured the mixture into the waiting vessel shouting, "Ta-dah!"

Margo felt like applauding but old Butterbrot was unimpressed. "I just wanted a strong drink," he frowned as he raised the glass and took a deep draught, "not a circus act."

Sport took his uniform coat from the peg and handed it to Margo along with his military cap. "Can you please hang these back in my office wardrobe?" he asked her.

When she returned, Mr. Butterbrot was sipping a fresh drink and petting a large ginger cat as Sport told him about the package that would be waiting back at his condo.

"I was too naive," Butterbrot told the barman, shaking his head. "I'd only just arrived here. I understood that the old spick ruled the island with an iron fist, so I assumed there wouldn't be any crime here. Boy was I in for a surprise." He took another long pull of gin. "If it ain't nailed down..." he drawled. The ginger tom seemed to nod agreement, its tail sweeping to-and-fro on the bar top.

"But it has finally arrived," Sport told him in an enthusiastic voice. Your big screen TV is here. I sent it up to your condo in the taxi myself."

"What," Butterbrot barked, "the mail is so slow here it takes Sony eight months to deliver a television? Better mix me another double. When the damn taxi's done delivering my flat screen TV, they can deliver me home." He thought for a minute, then added,

"Do you know some honest islander who can hook the damn thing up for me? I've been paying for the cable all this time to watch an old twenty-one inch box."

# Chapter Eleven

Margo awoke with a smile the next morning. She had her own coffee machine and a two pound bag of local beans that Sport had procured for her at next to nothing in cost. She gathered her novel notes along with her laptop and headed out to the terrace. On her second trip downstairs she brought a tall mug of strong coffee and some local pastry from the island bakery. Even the ferals patrolling the patio seemed to be smiling. This would be her best day of creating so far, how could it be anything else?

In the previous night, while drifting off to sleep, the lady had decided to pattern the principle character in her book on Sport. The man was an extremely cool cat with plenty of education. Was there anything Sport couldn't do? He was almost a Superman.

Careful, girl, she told herself. You don't want to fall for a drifter like this. But some other lobe of her brain disagreed. Who could be a better mate than this Banana Republic wildman?

Margo wrote a chapter or two, but in review she wasn't happy with her work. She took a break, checking up on New York friends via Facebook, then playing a few hands of Spider Solitaire. Finally out of fresh ideas, Margo closed her laptop, put it in her large straw handbag and headed down the hill to Sport's bar.

Junior Souza was there at the bar, half in the bag, pouring his heart out about how he was of pure blood but still, it seemed, could never be considered for the island's crown.

"Uncle Emmanuel wants his *daughter* to succeed him as the island's ruler," he laughed, "As though a woman could ever lead such an important island nation.

"I am the senior male child of the Souza family. Hell, I'm the only male child of my generation. By all that's right on earth and in heaven I should be the rightful heir to the throne. Even the padre of the Santa Nepenthe Cathedral agrees."

Sport brought Junior another double Bols gin and tonic. "I can dig what you're putting down," Sport told the royal child, "but your uncle *is* the supreme leader. It's hard to argue with that."

"Fuck my uncle," Junior screamed, then looked around the room, concerned as to who might have heard his comment. Cats ran to hide behind the bar.

"Hey, it's cool," Sport told him sotto voce. "I understand how you're feeling. But you've got to understand that life isn't always fair."

"So what am I supposed to do," Junior wailed as he pushed away the ginger cat that was trying to climb onto his lap.

"How about you get with all your family members that are talking about organizing a democratic election to determine who succeeds your Uncle Emmanuel? If your family will agree to place your name on the ballot, you might prove to be more popular than your cousin Amelia. It's probably your best shot."

Junior nodded and gave Sport a big smile just before he slid slowly from his stool onto the floor, the ginger tom climbing on his chest, purring and licking the man's face. Margo tried to revive the Supreme Leader's nephew by slapping his face a few times and pounding on his chest, but he was dead to the world. The ginger cat remained perched on Junior's chest and licked his face affectionately. Sport called the island taxi to take the man back to Vista Para o Mar. "You see what we're up against?" he chuckled at Margo.


Depressed by what she'd just witnessed, Margo ordered a double martini of her own, but with vodka rather that gin. She sat in silence as the taxi man shooed the cat away and dragged Junior Souza out by his heels while winking at Sport as though this was some kind of common joke.

Sport nodded as if to say, "Yeah, happens all the time."

"These are the kind of people that rule Santa Nepenthe?" Margo asked.

"Hey, what would you expect," Sport told her. "Four hundred years of inbreeding on a small rock with a limited gene pool in the first place? It still beats the heck out of nations that cow tow to the highest industrial bidder."

"That's nice," Margo replied, "but really, are we all that safe with this kind of leadership? And if so, how?"

"The island is safe because we don't have any natural resources, zero, zip," Sport laughed out loud. "No oil, no natural gas, no water… We have no reason why anyone would want to invade us… Unless they can figure out how to get energy out of bananas or pineapples."

"Cynical," was Margo's reply. "You are just being cynical."

"No," Sport replied, "I'm being realistic. Think about it."

"I'd rather not, thank you," Margo told him, upending her drink and slamming the empty glass on the bar with a look that said I'll need another and quickly.

Her glass was speedily refilled, Sport giving her a knowing grin. Margo was a bright girl, he thought, she just needed to open her eyes and lose some of her romantic idealism. The ginger cat climbed into her lap and began purring.

"So how's the book coming along?" Sport asked.

"Oh, I don't know," Margo answered, embarrassed that she was considering Sport for such a leading role in her writings. "Let's just say I've had a few new ideas that might work out."

"Ever thought of including a character patterned on me?" Sport asked with a wide grin, which caused Margo to choke on a swallow of vodka and lose her cool in a coughing fit. The cat slapped at her and tootled off down the bar. Einstein jumped up to take the ginger tom's place.

"So you have thought of it," the barman laughed with a wink.

"I won't have any more problems with packages mailed to me?" Margo asked to change the subject. She drummed her fingers on the bar to coax the feline closer.

Sport threw back his head and laughed loudly, "So I touched a nerve then? Hey, it's cool. I don't care if you write about me. You can even use my name."

Margo stared down at her laptop, not wanting to meet Sport's gaze. "Thanks for the drink," she told him in a soft voice. "I think I need to get back to the hotel."

"Hold on for just a minute and I'll make you some sandwiches so you can keep working through dinner," Sport told her.

Margo started to refuse the offer, then she thought better of it. "A couple sandwiches would be nice," she told the man coldly as she packed up her computer. "I'll see you tomorrow. Maybe I'll feel better then."

## ✺ Chapter Twelve ✺

Back at the Sovereign Hotel, Margo unpacked her computer, fired it up and connected to the Internet, but her mind seemed to be a total blank as far as continuing her story line. Sport would be a perfect protagonist, but in her current frame of mind she didn't want to let him know of her feelings toward him. Outside, the afternoon rain had started.

In a fit of pique, she emailed an on again, off again boyfriend in Manhattan and invited him to come and visit her for a week end. If nothing else, Rudy could catch her up on what was going on around the Manhattan social scene.

Well, in true fact, it would be closer to a week's visit. Either that or an overnight stay, depending on when Rudy might catch the supply boat out of San Juan and how long he might want to spend with her.

In the back of her mind, some soft voice told her she only wanted to make Sport jealous, but Margo ignored that voice, telling herself that she didn't really care what Sport might think.

When she finally turned off her laptop and turned back the sheets on her narrow bed, Margo had a sort of 'buyer's remorse' about the message she'd sent to Rudy.

Rudy was very self-absorbed and tended to be quite controlling, which was why she'd stopped dating him in the first place. But maybe, if Sport really cared for her, he would put Rudy in his place and send him back to New York with his tail between his legs.

Then again, is that what she really wanted? Life was so confusing.

Sunday morning, she slept late, making a strong coffee for herself in her room but heading down the hill after one cup. Sport was already behind the bar wearing his trade-mark casual grin.

"Hey, princess," he greeted her. "Feeling a little better today? I didn't mean to upset you with that crazy idea that I might be a character in your book. I apologize if I was out of line."

"No," Margo stuttered. "You kinda caught me off guard because I was thinking that very same thing, only I didn't want it to go to your head."

They both laughed as Sport set a coffee in front of her and laced it with some of the local island rum. The brown tabby, Einstein, was back seeking her attention.

"You know that I never intended to be any kind of local hero," the barman told her. "I've always just wanted to blend into the scenery and live a quiet life with no stress or hassles."

"That may be so," Margo told him. "And if I can help you in that I will. But it looks like we might be on the edge of something far bigger than either you or me. Let's just see where all this takes us."

To Sports confused face, Margo said, "Do you think Junior could be a serious candidate if they held a democratic election for the island? What's Junior's level of education? And if he should throw his name in the ring, what kind of chance would he stand of winning? Would the people really reject his sister just because of her sex? And are the islanders likely to be taken in by some American who says he wants to change everything?"

"Whoa, slow down a minute," Sport laughed. "Junior is full of ideas, but he doesn't carry much weight in island politics. His education is questionable as he's never been off the island, but his cousin Amelia could have tutored him some.

"But there won't be any kind of election unless old man Souza wants it. And yes, I think Santa Nepenthe's population is very primitive and male dominated. It would take a lot for them to consider a female leader, even if she is very intelligent and educated. The schools on the island only go up to the equivalent of about the eighth grade. The population is literate, as in they can read and write in both Portuguese and English, do simple math as it applies to buying and selling crops and understand seasons for planting and harvesting those crops, but that's about it. They have no need to study political science because the Supreme Leader takes care of all that business for them."

"But they have the Internet now," Margo protested, absent-mindedly stroking the tabby's soft white tummy. "Surely that is going to arouse their curiosity. They can now get information from Wikipedia and other educational sites. They can follow world politics, entertainment trends and learn about history…"

"Only if they're motivated to look for such things," Sport told her with a serious face. "But why would the common islander have an interest in such things. The entertainment trends maybe or world cup soccer, but history or global politics? What possible effect could these things have on their day-to-day life? The Supreme Leader cares for all his children, just as the priest tells them every Sunday that their savior does. They're double protected. What more could they need?"

Margo's head and shoulders dropped into a slump. "Oh God," she breathed. "I want to think you're being cynical again, but it makes too much sense, these poor people."

"Poor, maybe," Sport replied, "but they're happy. They don't know any different so they accept both their pleasures and their sorrows. Life is simple for the islanders. They grow food, they enjoy their natural surroundings, they make love and they pray. There's little worry about paying bills or besting their neighbors. Life is simple and life is good, just like it is for all these stray cats around here."

"But do they read books?"

"Mainly their Bibles," Sport answered quickly. "We don't have libraries or book stores on Santa Nepenthe. But we don't have gun shops either. Or car dealerships or big box stores. People buy from their neighbors to fill their needs, and their neighbors are crafts-men, carpenters, butchers and bakers. It's a balanced life."

"But what do they do for fun?" Margo inquired. No movies, no books to read…"

"We have local musicians that perform. Everyone on the island loves music and dance. And we have a great football club, what you call soccer in America. Our national team is always high in the island league. We regularly beat St Thomas and Martinique. We've even won against Jamaica a time or two."

"But how does your team get off the island to play these other clubs?" Margo wanted to know.

Sport laughed once more his full throated laugh. "Football is one of the island's top priorities. The Souza family has a special yacht dedicated to ferrying the Nepenthe Panthers to away games. Some of the best paid workers on the island are the sailors who crew the Panther's yacht."

Margo shook her head, then raised it high and said, "I think I need another strong coffee, only hold the coffee and put some coconut milk in the rum."

Sport complied with a smile and fixed a similar drink for himself, then poured a saucer of milk for the tabby cat which quickly brought more strays to the counter top.

## Chapter Thirteen

It turned out to be another wasted day. Margo drank rum with Sport after breakfast then, how many drinks later in the morning? One of the Souza daughters entered the bar wanting Sport to help her understand why island government was so difficult to figure out. Sport began lecturing the lady about the American Revolution and the failing US experiment with democracy.

After many hours of conversation, Sport and young Miriam Souza agreed to disagree about human nature and politics, in spite of both Sport and Margo putting forth some very sound arguments.

When Morais' island taxi had spirited a tipsy Miriam back to her condo, Sport rolled his eyes at Margo. "You see what we're up against?" he asked once again.

"Well, with no advanced education, what do you expect?" Margo replied. "Why doesn't Santa Nepenthe have a university, or even a junior college? The next generation needs to know something about the modern world out there."

"You're preaching to the choir," Sport replied. "Believe me, I've told O Cabeça many times that he needs to offer his subjects a better education, but I think he believes that education will cause people to question his leadership. He's terrified of subjects that might ask questions about his role as the island's leader. He won't even allow a high school here." Sport stroked the ginger tabby that tried to climb up his chest.

"Like I said," Margo gloated, "The man's a dictator."

"No, don't say that," Sport countered.

"But it's true," Margo shouted, "Open your eyes and look at the facts."

"Not so loud," Sport cautioned. "The walls have ears. They might have this place bugged. I don't know about you, but I don't want to swim to some other island."

Now it was Margo's turn to throw her head back in laughter. "You just confirmed what I said. If Souza wasn't a dictator, you wouldn't be so paranoid about speaking out."

From a low profile behind the bar, Sport whispered, "Souza doesn't have to be a dictator to be concerned about opposition. These are new and different times on the island. Wouldn't you be a bit cautious with so many new ideas finding their way to these shores? The natives went from no real news to Fox News, and they believe everything they see and hear. If it's on the Internet or television, it must be true. Don't you think Souza has some legitimate concerns? Wouldn't you?"

"Not if I was running an open and transparent government," Margo proclaimed loudly, her head held high.

Sport ducked farther behind the bar, the tabby on the edge of the counter staring down at him like a medieval gargoyle. "Not so loud," he whispered. "Don't you want to live to publish your novel?"

"I rest my case," Margo laughed. "I've never seen this scared side of you before, Sport. And I don't see any soldiers coming through the door to shut me up."

"Sure," Sport told her. "They won't grab you here in such a public location. They'll come for you in the night with chloroform rags and plastic ties and I'll never hear from you again. You aren't even one of us. Sure, America may have paperwork saying that you came here, but the government here will just say that they never saw you, or that you were here but you sailed off with someone they didn't know. You really shouldn't get involved in politics here, it just isn't healthy."

"And this from the man whose a Major in the island's army?"

"Hey, I know how to play the game..."

"Oh please," Margo countered. "This is the twenty-first century. The world is all pretty much connected and international questions would surely be asked if I was to suddenly disappear."

Sport sadly shook his head. "In Santa Nepenthe it's still the dark ages, believe me. You really don't understand what you're dealing with."

"I'm a journalist," Margo replied, head held high. "I'll get the word out if there is anything wrong. The world will read my words and pass judgment that will rock this tiny island nation."

Sport gave a hollow laugh. "I don't think you understand what you're dealing with here. You've led a sheltered life in a country where police can be trusted most of the time and public opinion holds a lot of sway. Santa Nepenthe isn't quite like that, no matter what you've been told. This island is a peaceful and safe place to live as long as you don't rock the boat. If you need to question the hierarchy, you are looking to get slapped down hard. Believe me, I've spent almost a third of my life here."

Margo tossed back the last of her drink. "I'll give that some thought," she told Sport. "Meanwhile, call me a cab and I'll grab a good night's sleep without any worry."

# ☙ Chapter Fourteen ☙

On entering Sport's establishment the next day, Margo was greeted by taxi cab driver Morais. "O Cabeça has requested that you might have breakfast with him at The Palace," the man smiled. Sport gave Margo a sad look from behind the bar. "I told you so," his drawn face seemed to say.

"Can I have a cup of coffee first?" Margo asked the taxi man, "and a few private moments to talk with my friend here?"

"It is not polite to keep the Supreme Leader waiting," Morais told her, "but I will turn my head away for a moment or two."

"What should I do?" Margo mouthed silently at Sport. The barman read her lips and shrugged his shoulders.

"Sport?" she queried aloud.

The barman laid an empty smile on her, as if to say, "I warned you."

"I'm sending an amazing breakfast up to the palace with you," he smiled. "Crab Benedict with Hollandaise and spiced fried potatoes, and a big jug of local coffee."

All kinds of bad thoughts ran through the lady journalist's mind. Pictures of her being thrown from high lava cliffs or her body being ravished by drunken low-life island soldiers. What have I gotten myself into she wondered. Margo followed Sport out to the waiting cab as he carried a dozen or more ceramic hot dishes in insulated bags which he placed in the old Ford's boot. Morais held open the front passenger door for her with a broad grin. He closed the door behind Margo when she was in place, then walked around to the driver's door, sat down and pressed his finger on the starter button.

As the taxi pulled away from the wharf, Morais turned to give Margo a big smile. "O Cabeça has heard some wonderful things about you," the man told her. "I think he may have a very good position to offer you in his government."

"But I don't want or need a job," Margo replied, wide eyed. "I work for an American newspaper and I'm only here to write a book."

"One does not argue with our Supreme Leader," the cabbie winked. "Most the people on our island would give everything they own to please Senhor Souza."

Margo found herself shivering in spite of the humid 82-degree heat outside. "I don't think I know enough about this island to be of any reasonable service."

"Ah," Morais countered, "but you have an education, just like Senhor Sport. Education is a very sought after commodity in our little island's government."

"What do you know about education?" Margo asked the man.

"My father was an off-islander," Morais replied. "He came here during World War II with the American forces. When my parents were divorced, I went to live with my father briefly in New York. I went to Kingsborough Community College in Brooklyn for one year. I learned enough that when I returned here, I was able to have this car imported from Cuba and start my own business, with the Souza's blessing, of course."

Margo continued to squirm in her seat. "So, what did you study?"

"Oh, business courses, yes, that and some broadcasting classes. I really wanted to start a radio station on Santa Nepenthe, but no one here had any interest, including the royal family. The government told me that a taxi cab would be a very big plus for the island, but a radio station would only be a waste of time."

At the gates of the Souza compound, two guards in uniforms similar to Sport's army reserve coat saluted and waved Morais's taxi through. These men had the same seagull and gourd logo on their hats, but in gray, rather than gold braid. Their grins frightened Margo. These men had empty eyes, killer's eyes that were not at all reassuring to her.

At the wide porte-cochere of the palace, Morais handed Margo off to another pair of white-uniformed giants. These men ogled her as if she was nothing but a piece of meat, but in the end they delivered her to the main hall of the Souza palace. Other soldiers followed carrying the breakfast dishes Sport had prepared.

At the entrance to the large room, a slender young lady with light brown hair greeted her. "Ms. Drelve?" the lady asked. "We are so glad that you have come to Santa Nepenthe. It is like a sign from the Gods, a sign that change must come our way. We have long awaited such a sign."

"Me?" Margo asked in a weak voice while looking around to be sure they weren't referring to someone standing behind her. 'Me?" she squeaked again, placing the palm of her left hand flat across her chest. "But I just came here to write a book. I have no idea about your island or your politics. I was just looking for a quiet place to kick back and write without a lot of bright lights or noise."

"But you are here now," said the lady. "It must be pre-ordained by God. Excuse me if I haven't introduced myself. I am Amelia, Emmanuel Souza's oldest daughter. My father and I hope that I will be the next Supreme Leader of our island. Of course, we understand that Santa Nepenthe is a male dominated society. It has been this way for some four-hundred years. But now we are learning from the Internet and other sources. We must hope that Hillary Clinton will convince our population that a woman can take responsibility for a large nation of people. She is our shining example for our future. We are all sure she will be America's next president."

"But what could I possibly do to help you?" Margo whined. "I'm not an island native or even a transplant. I'm only here visiting for a short while, until I complete my novel. It's not even a book about your island. I only came here for some peace and quiet. And now you seem to want to rob me of that. I think I'd be better off to go back to Yonkers to write my book."

"Please," begged Miriam, the younger daughter whom Margo recognized from the girl's drunken afternoon at Sport's. "I don't have the advantage of my sister's higher education, but I can clearly see how your knowledge could benefit our cause. All we need is for you to verify the facts in Amelia's campaign and stand against the falsehoods that off island news might present."

Margo hadn't a clue how to answer this, *falsehoods* from off the island? She sat pondering this for some two minutes in abject silence. Amelia finally broke the silence, asking one of the soldiers to bring Margo a glass of some local wine.

"So where did you go to college?" Amelia asked with an open curious face. "I did my seven years at Cal Berkeley. Living around the San Francisco bay area was sure an eye-opener for me after growing up on Santa Nepenthe. I think the Berkeley campus had more students than our island has citizens."

"I received my journalism degree from the State University of New York," Margo answered without a thought. "It was close to home. I was a sheltered Jewish girl and didn't want to travel far from my parents and friends." Margo took a glass of wine from the soldier that shimmered through the rear door holding a brass tray and bowed. After Margo took a sip and gave an approving nod, the man offered wine to both the royal sisters.

"A school close to home?" Amelia repeated as the soldiers began setting Sport's breakfast dishes out on the long table. Both daughters laughed at this. "I wish I could have found a school where I could be close to my friends," she confessed. "But in the end, I learned so much that I never had a clue about while growing up here on Santa Nepenthe. America was so very different from our special island. So many comforts those people enjoy. I even learned to drive a *car*. This is why I must succeed my father as Supreme Leader of our nation. I must lead my people into the twenty-first century or we will surely disappear from the globe."

"But you have the Internet here," Margo pointed out. "Some folks here even have televisions."

"The rich off-islanders in Vista Para o Mar have television, maybe also a handful of our better off citizens. There are not so many televisions on the island," Miriam assured her.

"I'll bet you have televisions here in the palace," Margo chuckled.

"We have had this for many years," Amelia replied in a haughty tone. "It is imperative that my father keeps up on world affairs. You must understand this."

Margo's chuckle matured into a full and loud laugh. "Of course I understand. I wasn't trying to offend anyone, but I'll bet you watch TV yourself."

"We live in Vista Para o Mar," Miriam pointed out. "Only my father and his servants live here in the palace. It is a big building, yes, but remember, it is also the center of our government. Many officials have their offices on the ground floor of this building."

"And," Amelia added, "We only have Internet and satellite TV on Santa Nepenthe because I discovered these things when I lived in California. When I returned from Berkeley, I convinced my father that our island needed these things available to all our people, that it would be a good thing for progress."

"Well," Miriam confessed, "a few of the off islanders living in our condominium project had computers and televisions already, but they paid a very high price for their private satellite hook-ups, just as did our father."

"The units in Vista Para o Mar were much easier for our government to sell to rich tourists," Amelia added, "once we had free Internet and cheap TV hook-ups."

"How long have you had telephones here?" Margo asked. "I noticed the public phone sign on the front of Sport's bar looks quite old and faded.

"The American navy set up a very primitive telephone network during the great war," Amelia told Margo. "It was to help the defense of all the surrounding islands. But that was long before I was born. When I was a child, our father upgraded our telephone lines with the help of Senhor Morais, the taxi cab man. Senhor Morais was quite knowledgeable about such things as he had studied radio at school in America. He ordered much new equipment for our island with the help of his father in New York. Morais is still the man we call if there is a problem with our phones. You might say the taxi company is also our telephone company."

"For which he is generously compensated," Miriam put in. "O Cabeça takes good care of those who help him." She took a sip of her wine.

"And," Amelia reminded Margo, "O Cabeça wants you to help him, to help us all. You should at least hear us out on this. I'm sure you could assist us and still have plenty of free time to write on your novel."

"Father might even find quarters for you here in the palace and get you out of that terrible hotel in the city."

"I'm quite happy at the Sovereign Hotel," Margo sneered. "Besides, I thought no one lived here but your father. And where is your mother, may I ask?"

Both girls went deathly quiet. Margo shifted her eyes from one lady to the other as the silence dragged on. The sister's faces were like granite, their eyes dark and cold.

## 🌴 **Chapter Fifteen** 🌴

Finally Miriam let out a deep sigh and Amelia whispered, "We do not ever speak of our mother. I can only say that she was a traitor to Santa Nepenthe." Miriam began to weep softly.

"I, I'm sorry," Margo stuttered. "I didn't know. I apologize for bringing her up."

Miriam bit her lower lip and whispered, "She broke our father's heart. No one is ever to break the heart of a nation's Supreme Leader."

Amelia turned and folded her younger sister in her arms, patting her back and breathing soft words into the younger girl's ear. Miriam nodded and Amelia turned back toward Margo.

"Please, never mention our mother to anyone. Not even your friend who owns the bar or any of your acquaintances back in America. We *must* think of her as dead.

"She ran away with an off-islander," Miriam confided in a voice quiet and husky from crying. "This devil came to Santa Nepenthe looking to buy a vacation condo. He never bought any property here, but he stole our mother from us. She lives in Paris now…"

"She is **dead**!" hissed Amelia abruptly, standing and pulling at her neatly coifed hair. "She lives nowhere." And with that, the woman drained the remaining wine in her glass and threw the vessel at the wall where it shattered into a hundred small shards.

A silence stretched broken only by the heavy breathing of the royal sisters. Soon, a solder glided into the room with a fresh tray of wine glasses and a newly opened bottle. He passed out drinks, touched the side of his nose with the index finger of his free hand and told the girls, "I heard nothing." Sport's fine food sat on the table before them but remained untouched.

Amelia sat back down in her chair, shook her head violently side-to-side, then turned her face up wearing a smile. "Please," she said, "Let us return to the business we are here to discuss. I have convinced father that we should hold free and democratic elections next year. You, Margo, will help me present convincing arguments why the people should vote for me and only me. This should be easy for you with your study of journalism."

Margo's face clouded. "But who on this island is qualified to run against you? I would think you would easily win any democratic contest. Are there others among the island population who have been to a college or university anywhere?"

"We live in a male oriented society," Amelia reminded Margo. "The people of Santa Nepenthe strongly believe that only a man would be qualified to rule. We are a very devout Catholic people. Our Savior, Jesus Christ, was a man. Our Pope is a man. My father and all our Supreme Leaders before him were men. We may be living in new times, but much of our population would not accept such a thing as a female leader."

"What?" Margo ejaculated. "I don't understand how this could…"

"You have noted yourself that we have no higher education on Santa Nepenthe," Miriam lamented. "How could our people accept new ideas that they've never been exposed to? I am only somewhat educated because my big sister has tutored me and shown me how to research information on the Internet."

"But, Amelia, do you have any serious competition if such an election should take place?" Margo asked.

"Unfortunately, I have," Amelia told her. "We have one or two off-islanders residing in Vista Para o Mar who would love to exploit our island under the guise of bringing us progress."

Miriam nodded vigorously and uttered a single word, "Friend."

"Friend?" Margo parroted.

"We have a neighbor in our condo community," Amelia sighed. "His name is Alphonse Ameche, but he is known to all as 'Friend.' He is also from New York, but I don't believe he is any kind of friend to our island."

"He is an opportunist," Miriam barked. "He would enslave our people, I am sure of it."

"And he's thrown his hat in the election ring?" Margo asked.

Both sisters laughed. "More than that," Amelia told Margo. "He is telling our people he will bring money and jobs to Santa Nepenthe. He is telling our neighbors in Vista Para o Mar that he will build big hotels and casinos across the unspoiled nature of our island's north shore. He is even talking about an airport right in the middle of our richest farming plateau."

"An airport," Margo echoed, "And casinos? Doesn't the world have enough casinos?"

"I know very little about casinos," Amelia confided. "But I spent a week end in Las Vegas once on spring break from college.

I would never want our island to look like this place; the flashing lights, the noise, the crazy drunken people. How could such a thing be viewed as progress?" Amelia took another sip of her wine and the other girls followed suit.

"I think it would only be viewed as *profits*," Margo chuckled. "If it's true, somebody is looking to milk your island paradise for their own personal gain."

The royal sisters stared at Margo. "Personal gain?" they asked in unison.

"Casinos bring in horrendous amounts of money," Margo explained, "Money for the men that *own* the casino. Sure, they may hire locals to work for them and pay those folks more money than they've ever made before, but the bulk of the money they bring in will never be seen by the people of Santa Nepenthe. It will surely be sent somewhere off island leaving your nation almost as poor as when you started."

## ❦ Chapter Sixteen ❦

Senhor Morais ferried Margo back to Sport's bar that afternoon, after two or three bottles of island wine with the ladies at the palace. The breakfast Sport had prepared had gone untouched. Margo was angry and fired up. She really had no interest in Santa Nepenthe, per se, but she was extremely angry that some American business man would want to stick his nose in local politics and spoil such a primitive paradise. Who did this Ameche character think he was, anyway? Taking her place at the bar, she was comforted by the brown tabby cat, Einstein, who seemed to love her. She stroked the animal and took some deep breathes to try and calm herself.

Over a few Mojitos, (who was counting?) she relayed her visit with the royal sisters to Sport. There were a handful of locals celebrating a birthday in the back of the bar, so her encounters with Sport were broken and jagged. Finally, just after nine, the birthday table settled up and headed out into the humid night.

"So, have you been listening to me?" she asked the bar man with clouded, red eyes.

"Yeah, I've caught a bit of your drift," Sport chuckled. "And I know Friend. He has meals and booze catered up to his place from time to time. Morais says he seems to be a good egg. So what's the problem?"

"This man says he intends to run against Princess Amelia for the post of Supreme Leader. He's talking about building an airport and gambling casinos."

"Welcome to the Banana Republics," Sport laughed. "All the losers find their way down here with their big dreams. This guy is full of talk but let's see where he stands if there really *is* an election. I wouldn't worry about it."

"Wouldn't worry about it," Margo roared. "What if these people, who've discovered materialism on the Internet, take him seriously and believe he'll have good paying jobs for all of them?"

"The whole idea of a democratic election here is pretty far-fetched," Sport chuckled. "Old man Souza says a lot of crazy things, but his ideas change from day to day. A week from now he probably won't even remember that he suggested an election."

Margo left the bar in a huff. She was so angry she actually stormed up the hill to her hotel on foot carrying her laptop bag to let off some steam. Once in her room, she made her Internet connection and did a search for sites that gave background checks for criminal activity, outstanding debts and family history.

Margo typed in A. Friend and New York. 'Alphonse Ameche' immediately popped up, alias Al Friend. Born to Italian immigrant parents in New York City in 1947, Alphonse Ameche dropped out of high school in Brooklyn and took a job with a company that placed juke boxes and cigarette machines in local bars from New York up through the Boston area. In 1986, he legally changed his name to Al Friend, an Americanization of his Italian name. He was suspected in a number of RICO cases over the next decade, but never convicted. He began buying and selling real estate, which was believed to be a cover for laundering drug money. Much of the questionable funds he handled were invested in hotels and restaurants. When the IRS began an investigation into Friend's taxes, the man disappeared off the radar. Authorities suspected the man might have fled to Brazil or some other nation with no extradition treaties from where he was running his empire through old family connections in America.

Margo slept well that night, closing her eyes with a satisfied smirk. Now she had some ideas on how she might help Amelia if there was an election. Nobody would want a mob connected Italian criminal as Supreme Leader of their land.

The next morning, on entering Sport's establishment for breakfast, she asked the man, "When did Friend come to Santa Nepenthe?"

"I think it was in the mid-1990s," he replied. "It was just a few years after I landed here."

Margo opened her laptop and fired it up on the bar. When she had connected to the World Wide Web, she made a face of concentration toward her computer screen, pushed a few keys, and then looked up at Sport. "That's just about the time the American IRS started looking into this 'Friend' guys business dealings."

Sport chuckled. "So I'm not the only one that's…"

"That's not funny," Margo barked. "You were avoiding unfair drug laws that singled out folks they considered to be smugglers. It sounds like this man is a serious criminal, probably mafia connected, a *made* man, and he has been committing extremely illegal acts, like laundering drug money. And now this man wants to take control of our island paradise?"

"Babe," Sport replied, "From what you've told me over the past few months, you don't really think of this as a paradise. You said yourself that you miss having a supermarket, dance clubs and de-cent five-star restaurants." Sport gently lifted two stray cats off his food prep table and set them on the floor behind the bar.

"Damn it," the woman exploded, "Santa Nepenthe might just be the last place of its kind in this hemisphere. A supermarket and a disco might be nice accoutrements, but we certainly don't need ca-sinos or resort hotels. Or a bloody big airport that dumps hundreds of tourists here every day."

Sport roared with laughter at Margo's outburst. "You really think someone is going to spend millions of dollars to build such things on a lump of volcanic rock that doesn't even have a source of fresh water? They'd have to be crazy. We barely catch enough rain to water crops and hydrate our population as it is. Big tourist hotels would require thousands of gallons of fresh water daily."

"Are you sure of this?" Margo asked. "Maybe Friend plans to build a desalinization plant as well?"

"Throwing more good money after bad," Sport chuckled. "Think what the man would be paying the islanders in labor costs alone, and to import concrete, wood and steel from some other place. I think this guy is just blowing a lot of smoke. Where would some retired guy living in a banana republic condo come up with this kind of cash?"

"But if he's mob connected?" Margo questioned.

"Then he'd better have a pretty good story ready to convince even the hardest criminal organization to invest in this place," Sport said with a serious face. "The Mafia are businessmen. They're in business to make money, not to throw it after pipe dreams. I don't think the Souza's have anything to worry about."

## Chapter Seventeen

D ays drifted by and Margo fell back into her routine of writing most of the day and taking meals at Sport's Bar. When the weather was especially nice, as in not too hot or humid, she would go to the beach for a few hours, walk along the shoreline and then spread her towel and sunbathe. Many of her best book ideas came from these relaxing sessions. When she felt pressed for time, Margo would simply walk down to the strip of sand by the wharf, but when she felt she really needed some inspiration, she would call Senhor Morais to drive her to the broader sand of the north shore. Margo would unload her small web-backed chair, towel and laptop and then ask Morais to return for her at his convenience before the afternoon downpour began.

After her beach time on these days, she would have the taxi man drop her at the bar, without showering or changing, and she'd sound her day's new ideas off Sport while she got a solid buzz on before returning to her hotel.

Then one afternoon, Morais dropped Margo on the north shore to discover a scarlet and blue umbrella with the seagull and gourd of Santa Nepenthe setting on her favorite patch of sand.

"We haven't talked in awhile," Amelia said casually as Margo came around to the front of the large, round canopy. "I thought this might be a good time."

"But how did you know I'd be coming to the beach?" queried Margo.

"We know these things," laughed Amelia. "Santa Nepenthe is a small island."

Margo turned with an angry face. "Have you been spying on me?"

"Spying is such an ugly word," Amelia chuckled. "You are a valuable person-of-interest, a special tourist here. It is my government's responsibility to keep an eye on you. We wouldn't want any sort of unpleasantness that might upset our neighbors to the north."

"You've been spying on me." Margo loosed in an angry shout. "Your damn taxi man is telling you everywhere I go."

"Please, Margo. How do you Americans say? Lighten *up*. You are a strange bird on our island. Many people notice you wherever you go. Me, I'm mainly concerned for your safety. But I also think it is time we talked further about our island's upcoming election. Do you have anything new to report to me?"

"Oh, so now *I'm* one of your spies as well," Margo shouted, hands on her hips.

Amelia laughed again. "Oh, aren't we sensitive today? I thought we were friends? You sure didn't mind drinking my wine which, by the way, I brought a few bottles with me this beautiful morning. Why don't you just set that chair you're carrying next to mine and we can talk for awhile. Or we could take a little walk down the beach?"

Margo took a series of deep breaths to calm herself. "Okay," she finally told the royal daughter, forcing her face into a smile. "I suppose I do owe you the courtesy.

"I did some research on the Internet about this Friend guy. He's a criminal, plain and simple."

"Oh, we know all about that," Amelia smiled bringing a bottle from her bag, pulling the cork and pouring the vino into a couple of real crystal glasses. "Father's intelligence people figured that out when he was buying property on the island."

"So then you can stop him from running in your election," Margo nodded.

"Well," Amelia replied, "It just isn't that simple. We've never had a free election on Santa Nepenthe before. All our island criminals are exiled or hung, which protects us from such bad *island* people. But it leaves a big loophole in our laws. And the man *does* own property here, even if only a large condominium, which technically makes him a subject... or I guess we could say, a citizen. And he's never committed any crime against our island's people or government."

"There's a loophole that allows known criminals to run for office?"

"It's not exactly that," Amelia answered with a puzzled face, "More like since we've never had a free election, we have no laws what-so-ever about who can or cannot run for an office. The only law that's close is the one that says the leader of our people will be succeeded by his eldest child. I'm not even sure if it specifies 'eldest *male* child' as that issue has never come up before in our history.

The two ladies sipped red wine in silence for some time. Finally Margo asked, "Your father can't just make some new laws to cover this situation?"

"I wish he could. But father says that would not be fair. Government shouldn't be interfering in island life any more than it has to. He still sees himself as the benevolent father watching over all his children. That's what the people of Santa Nepenthe are to him, his children."

"Even the ones who come here from the outside world and might want to take advantage of the others?"

"Them especially," Amelia told Margo, shaking her head. "Father believes that as they observe the simple but beautiful life we live all around them, their hearts will open and they will become happy and simple as we are. Father Roboza in the cathedral agrees with him."

Margo rolled her eyes in frustration. "But this Friend guy is probably planning to destroy this very beach where we're sitting to build a huge hotel and casino."

"Yes, and an airport in the middle of our most fertile farm land, we talked about this before. What still remains is for you to help me find the words that can defeat this man."

Margo drained half her glass of wine in one swallow. "I'm as baffled as you are," she told the royal daughter. "I'll have to give this some deep thought."

Amelia turned from her beach chair, leaned over and gave Margo a big hug. "I know you will find the words. I could tell when I first laid eyes on you that you would be the one to save our island."

## ☆ Chapter Eighteen ☆

Margo and Amelia finished both bottles of wine between them without coming to any real conclusions. Morais returned just before the afternoon downpour began. He tied Amelia's umbrella on the roof of his taxi as he loaded both ladies' beach gear into the trunk of the old Ford. Morais told Amelia he would drop her at her condo before taking Margo into Cidade Sebastian, but the girl told him, "No. I think I want to go to the bar with my friend Margo." Morais gave questioning looks in the car's review mirror, but Amelia stared back with a face of stone. This was most unusual.

The two ladies mounted stools in the bar. Sport approached with a wide grin. "This is indeed an honor," he said with a deep bow, "A Princess and an American journalist."

"Can it," Amelia told him, looking around to see who might have heard their introduction. There was only Captain Moore and two of his sailors at a table in the back and they were beyond remembering much. Einstein, the tabby cat jumped up, licked Margo's hand and then went to rub his head on Amelia's arm.

"We're just two ladies out for an afternoon of fun," Margo told Sport with a wink. "Shall we have a couple martinis?" she asked her new friend.

"I don't think I've ever had a martini," Amelia replied wide eyed.

"Trust me, you'll like it," Margo told her tipping her head toward Sport. "Make'm gin doubles."

Sport brought the orange Bols bottle out from beneath the bar with a questioning look. Did he dare get the number one royal daughter squiffy? Amelia had seldom come into his place and when she did she never drank more than a few glasses of red wine. Margo winked at him, as if to say it was cool and she'd take responsibility.

Sport poured the ingredients into his silver shaker with a worried expression but when Margo winked his way again, he went into his usual martini mixing routine, tossing the olives, catching them in the glass and juggling the martini shaker in the air before pouring.

Amelia, already buzzed from drinking wine all day at the beach, was mesmerized. "Wow," she exclaimed, "you are so talented." she told Sport, leaning over the bar with moony eyes and her chin resting on the back of her intertwined fingers. "It's no wonder father thinks so highly of you."

Margo elbowed the royal daughter. "It's an act of seduction," she said loudly, "Don't fall for his charm."

The two ladies burst into giggles and sipped at their strong drinks. "Wow, this is refreshing," Amelia chortled, then took another swallow.

"Watch yourself," Margo replied again digging an elbow into the royal daughter's side. "This isn't simple wine we're dealing with here."

Amelia took another guzzle and both ladies burst into more giggles. Einstein laid down on the bar between them and went to sleep.

They engaged in small talk about school days and old boy-friends. Margo described her on again, off again, relationship with Rudy, who sold advertising for the newspaper where she worked. Amelia, with a demure look spoke of a rich California boy that she had dated at Berkeley. "His parents owned a vineyard in northern California," She confessed. "Ralph taught me everything I know about good wine."

They ordered more martinis, their laughter increasing as they sipped.

Around seven in the evening, Margo asked just what Amelia would require of her if she was to help with the campaign, but by then the royal girl's head was severely twisted. Amelia kept throwing her arms around Margo, drunkenly hugging her and telling her that she loved her as much as she loved her own blood sister.

Morais was summoned shortly there-after to take the Princess home. Amelia insisted that Margo accompany her in the island taxi, but by the time they reached Vista Para o Mar, Amelia was softly snoring. Margo supported her royal friend as she walked Amelia to her apartment door. Morais drove Margo back to her hotel. "No charge," he told her. "I will bill this to the government." Margo gave him a generous tip anyway and thanked him for bringing her friend home safely.

The next morning Sport scolded Margo. "You, my friend, are dicing with death, getting the number one daughter drunk out of her skull. What were you thinking?"

"Just that I need to girl-on-girl bond with her if we're going to make any progress here. Besides, didn't young Ms. Souza seem to have a good time?" Margo stroked the brown tabby that had become her number one buddy.

"She was having a good time, alright," Sport laughed. "But how's she feeling this morning? And which one of us is she likely to blame for a raging hangover like she's never known before?"

"Amelia is a Cal-Berkeley girl," Margo smiled. "Maybe she's never had any martinis, but I'll just bet that she's had a few hungover mornings. Don't you remember your days at UCLA?"

Sport laughed loudly. "Okay, I get your point," he replied. "I just have never thought of the Supreme Leader's daughter in that light. So do you want to call her this morning to make sure she's alright? I wouldn't want old man Souza coming down here to ask questions."

As if on cue, the telephone behind the bar rang. Sport eyed it suspiciously but Margo picked it up.

"Santa Nepenthe Bar," she purred, "Margo speaking. How can I assist you?"

"Margo," came the excited voice across the line. "I'm so glad I caught you there. I was calling to ask Sport how I could get a hold of you. I wanted to thank you for a wonderful evening. I can't remember when I've had so much fun. We must get together again, and soon. I need to introduce my little sister, Miriam, to those martini drinks. Wow, what a buzz. Will you be at Sport's place later this afternoon?"

"I'm not sure," Margo replied with a look at Sport. "I need to get in touch with my publisher," she lied, "How about tomorrow?"

"Tomorrow would be fantastic," Amelia replied without hesitation. "Do we want to do the beach first? I'd love to catch some more rays, as they say."

"No," Margo told her. "I need to get some more writing done on my book before I head down to the bar. Let's plan to meet at Sport's place around three, just before the rain starts."

# Chapter Nineteen

The three girls were on their third martinis, suffering severe giggling fits when Sport's phone rang. The aging hippie answered in his usual casual tone and then suddenly sprang to attention. "Yes sir!" he barked. Then, "Yes, sir, they're right here, all of them. Do you want to speak to Amelia?"

Sport listened again briefly then held to phone out to Margo. "*O Cabeça,*" he whispered.

"Father?" Miriam choked. "Does he know we're here?"

"We can be anywhere we like," Amelia reassured her sister, patting the girl's hand, but Miriam didn't look reassured.

Margo took the receiver and lifted it to her ear. "Senhor Souza," she purred, "I'm honored that you should call me." The she listened for some time while both Sport and the man's daughters gave her worried looks.

"Of course, I'd be honored," Margo replied at last. "I'm at your service whatever time is good for you." Another moment passed before Margo said. "Tomorrow at noon would be fine. I'll see you then."

Margo handed the telephone back to Sport with a smile. "Senhor Souza wants to talk to me," she smiled. "At noon tomorrow," she added.

"What did father want?" Miriam asked with a frightened look. "Did he mention us, I mean Amelia and me?"

"Only that Amelia told him she was impressed after our, uh, breakfast the other day. He said he'd like to discuss the idea of a free election with me." Margo stroked the snoozing tabby stretched out along the bar. "He told me that he would value my opinion highly."

Amelia nodded at her with a smile while Miriam breathed a sigh of relief. "This calls for a round on the house," Sport grinned, fetching the Bols bottle from under the bar.

Margo was a little nervous the next day when Morais called at the hotel for her. She hadn't packed anything formal to wear as she had intended to be either relaxing on the beach or holed up somewhere with her computer throughout her leave time on Santa Nepenthe. She finally chose to wear her best Hawaiian shirt, the one with the parrots and pineapples on it, and white slacks to the interview. Fortunately, both were clean and semi-pressed.

Senhor Morais was in a good mood, grinning widely at her in the rearview mirror. "You are suddenly very popular with our Supreme Leader and his family, Ms. Margo," he said with a wink. "I think it is good that you came to our island, no?"

"Yes, I think it might be good," Margo replied speculatively. "So far it has been good for my writing... You've lived in New York and you have some college, what do you think of the government on Santa Nepenthe? I mean honestly. I won't criticize your opinions or tell anyone else what you say, so be candid with me."

"Santa Nepenthe has been very good to me," Morais replied hesitantly. "What can I say?"

"Of course it has," Margo smiled back. "But is it good for *all* the people here? Does everyone have a good life? Do they all get enough to eat and good medical care? Things like that."

"Well, you must understand," Morais told her apologetically, "We do not have any doctors on our island. But our people are very healthy. We don't have what you call 'junk food.' All our food is organic, as you say. It all comes from the earth or from the surrounding waters."

Margo noticed that the taxi man was taking a longer, more scenic route to the top of the island. It appeared that he wanted to talk further with her before her appointment.

"What happens if one of your people here does get sick? How do you care for them?"

"That's a good question." The taxi man's face looked thoughtful in the mirror. "After the great war, we had a man who was, what did he call himself? A corpsman in the American navy, petty officer Mayhew. This man fell in love with an island girl, and after the war he returned here and married her. He set up a clinic in Cidade Sebastian where he treated anyone with cuts, coughs or sick children. He also told our Supreme Leader that we should have some kind of sick house for people who might have serious illnesses, so they did not spread illness to their neighbors.

"At petty officer Mayhew's urging, O Cabeça entered into an agreement with the island of Virgin Gorda, some thirty miles away. There is an old British hospital on Virgin Gorda, very well staffed. We are permitted to send anyone with a serious health problem to this hospital. We send them on the island football club's yacht, which is the fastest boat on the island."

"So Mr. Souza really *does* care for everyone as though they were his own children."

"Oh yes," Morais replied with enthusiasm. "This is true. O Cabeça cares about every one of us."

"What about the money the Souza family gets from selling condos to off-islanders or the fees they charge for cable Internet service?"

"Much of this is what we pay for things like using the hospital on Virgin Gorda as well as to pay our public servants. Only the very wealthy of Santa Nepenthe pay taxes. The only realistic property tax here is that charged on the condominiums of Vista Para o Mar. The farm land and the villages all belong to the people of Santa Nepenthe, so their contributions are small."

Margo noticed that they were now back on the main road heading for the Souza Palace. She smiled at Senhor Morais in his driving mirror. "Thank you for talking to me," she told him sincerely. "I appreciate your opinion."

"Não é nada." Morais replied.

## Chapter Twenty

This time, when the taxi pulled under the porte-cochere, the soldiers who greeted Margo were extremely polite, fawning over her and holding the door open. They even bowed to her as she entered the palace.

Emmanuel Souza was waiting behind a broad desk made of dark wood in his private office at the head of the stairs. The officers steered Margo to a deep brocade lounger set at an angle before Souza's desk. Another man in uniform set a tray on the small table beside the chair containing a large glass carafe of coffee along with a white china creamer and sugar bowl.

"It was so good of you to come," Souza said, standing briefly and bowing as Margo was seated. "We are honored by your presence on our humble island. Please enjoy some coffee. It is our locally grown specialty. And the sugar also is grown and refined right here on Santa Nepenthe."

The soldier standing by handed Margo a cup and poured when she nodded yes. "No cream or sugar," she told the man. "I'll savor the natural flavor."

When the coffee was poured, the man faded somewhere into the back of the room where he stood at parade rest with the other two soldiers awaiting further instruction.

The Supreme Leader was a portly man with iron gray hair worn just a bit long, but neatly combed back over his high forehead. The man wore a pencil-thin mustache like a line drawn along his upper lip and a bright white military-style tunic with gold braided shoulder boards. His hands, resting on the desk, were large with peppercorn clumps of gray hair reaching down towards his well manicured nails.

"So, my daughters are quite impressed with you," Souza stated through a thousand-candle-power smile. "They tell me you are more than just well educated. They say you are extremely smart as well."

Margo blushed silently at the compliment. "No, really," Souza assured her. "It is quite fortuitous that you have come to our small island nation at this time. It is a time of change for us here. A time for growth and betterment, I hope."

Margo sipped her coffee while keeping eye contact with the man.

"You'll excuse me if I don't express myself so well. I am a humble man without my oldest daughter's advantage of a college degree."

"You're doing fine, Senhor Souza... May I address you as Senhor Souza?"

The Supreme Leader burst into laughter. "We must become good friends, Ms. Margo. Please call me Manny. That is how those close to me here address me. It is what my father always called me when no one else was around and I kind of like the sound of it."

Margo was momentarily at a loss for words. It felt strange indeed to suddenly be on a first-name basis with a dictator or whatever this man was. The man's daughters felt comfortable as friends, but this man held the power of life and death over an entire island of his subjects.

Sensing Margo's discomfiture, Emmanuel Souza threw his arms wide, palms up and told her, "What can I say? I'm just a man. A man that by a twist of luck or fate was gifted with a small nation of wonderful people to care for, and I love them all. So tell me, please, is it time for me to ask my children to decide their own fate? Is it time for my island to hold these, what Amelia calls, 'free elections' to decide who will care for my people after I am gone?"

"But you look strong and fit to me," Margo told the man. "Is it important that someone is chosen to follow in your legacy just yet?"

The Supreme Leader's head slumped and his face went into a frown. "Please," he whispered, "Say nothing to my daughters. The doctor who comes to check me from the Virgin Gorda hospital, he tells me that I have something he calls a tumor growing on my brain and that I may not live beyond a few more months. It is time right now to decide who shall take my place. I go to our cathedral daily and pray that I might keep my wits about me and live long enough to see my daughter Amelia accepted as my successor. But at the same time, I feel I should give all my children the right to decide who they would have lead them into this bright new future. Does this make sense?"

Margo thought about all she had just heard for a minute or more before answering. "Senhor... Manny, this is sad and surprising news indeed. So no one knows of your illness?"

"No one but Dr. Roberts from Virgin Gorda, who has promised to keep my secret so that there is no panic on our island. Above all else, I do not want my daughters to know."

"I can understand," Margo told the man. "This is quite a situation."

Senhor Souza smiled weakly. "So you understand my dilemma. In light of this, is it a good thing to hold these elections? And if I do so, what chance do I have that my children will choose to have my daughter carry on after me?"

"Elections are always a gamble," Margo mused. "Like a horse race… do you know what a horse race is?"

Souza smiled again. "I have bet on horses a time or two when I've traveled off our island. It does not sound so promising."

"But it can be if we can make Amelia sound good enough to your people. The islanders have to be assured that the Souza blood running in her veins plus the years of schooling she accomplished will be the key to a brighter future full of progress."

"Yes," old Souza nodded. "This is exactly what I have been thinking. So you will help Amelia to win this election if I schedule it?"

"I'll do what I can, Manny," she told the man. "But I don't really know or understand your island or its culture. I'll have to rely on my knowledge of human nature."

"I think that will be good," he told her with an ear-to-ear grin. "You do your best. And if you have any questions, please call me any time of day or night. My servants will give you my private phone number here at the palace. If it is not so urgent, just tell my daughters."

Margo agreed that she would.

"But please, I beg of you, never tell them that I am ill. I suppose one day I won't be able to hide it from them, but for now, I'd rather they did not know."

# Part II

# Royal Friendships

## Chapter Twenty-One

"Υou are very quiet, my friend," Morais said, looking into the taxi's mirror. "Did O Cabeça say something that has upset you?"

"Do you call him Manny?" Margo replied to his question. The taxi man squirmed a bit in his seat. "Well, we *are* very old friends…" he offered in an apologetic tone. "But I would never address O Cabeça in this manner in front of other island people. When my father was stationed here during the war, he became good friends with our leader, uh, Manny. Then my father returned to America. Manny was kind to my mother when my father divorced her and he treated me like a son.

"Then I chose to return here after my year of college. Our leader took a great interest in me. He listened to my dreams of building a radio station on Santa Nepenthe and he counseled me. He paid for the car that I still maintain and drive to serve our people. I guess I have earned the right to call him Manny. I love our leader as I loved my father. He is a great man."

Margo slowly clapped her hands in the back seat of the cab. "That was a very moving speech," she told him watching Morais blush in the rearview mirror. "No, I really mean it," she assured him. "Even though the man speaks of all the island population as his children, I wouldn't imagine that many folks get truly close to the man. It's good that you and I can talk like this. I value your opinion because his daughters, well, they're his daughters so they would naturally have a high opinion of their father. Sport, the barman, tells me some things about Manny, but I don't believe they know each other that well…"

"Make no mistake," the taxi man stated emphatically, "Mr. Sport knows O Cabeça *very* well. Who do you think Manny turned to when his wife disappeared? I know it is forbidden to discuss this on our island, but it is a fact of life, an undeniable truth that the man's wife deserted him. In his darkest hour, Manny turned to strong drink for a short while and during that time, Sport was O Cabeça's closest friend. She was a beautiful woman, maybe half Manny's age…"

"Please, don't say any more," Margo pleaded as the cab pulled up in front of Sport's place. "This is more information than I need. By the way, how old is Manny?"

"I believe our Supreme Leader was born just before the Great War, probably in the mid 1930s. I myself was born in 1947, not long after the Americans left our little island. I was a boy of nine or ten when Manny's father suddenly fell over and died. Petty Officer Mayhew, who was still on Santa Nepenthe at that time, says that the old man's heart quit beating. It was a sad time for us."

"So you must be close to seventy," Margo stated as she reached into her purse for money.

"Please, this trip is on O Cabeça, Ms. Margo," the man told her with downcast eyes.

"That may be," Margo told him, "but you have been extremely helpful to me. I think you've earned a substantial tip. And I hope we can talk again. Speaking with you is always enlightening."

# Friend

The MV Dexter had arrived only moments before and Sport was busy pulling beers and mixing drinks for Captain Moore and his crew. Margo took her usual stool and greeted the ginger tabby that she had started calling John Lennon, or John-boy for short. She confided to the footloose feline that her life was getting busier than she had planned and asked the maugy to give her what comfort he could. John-boy began to purr loudly. "I'm glad we understand each other," Margo told him. A jealous Einstein watched from the back corner of the bar.

When all the ship's crew was settled with drinks and food in front of them, Sport came over to where Margo was sitting. "So, anything enlightening from O Cabeça?" he asked.

"You were the man's therapist and counselor when his wife left," she answered with hooded eyes. "I'll bet there's a lot you could tell me about the man."

Sport stared to choke. "It's forbidden to talk about..." he coughed.

"I know that," Margo giggled.

"Ah, something like doctor-patient confidentiality maybe?" Sport continued in a weak voice.

"Oh, so you're a psychiatrist now too," she laughed.

Sport mechanically brought out an Estonian vodka bottle from under the bar and took a pull directly from the vessel, then wiped the neck with his hand and poured Margo a shot.

"I could get disappeared if anyone hears me talking about, ah, you know what." The barman's hands were shaking. He took another hit directly from the bottle, bringing the level of the liquid seriously lower.

It was Margo's turn to laugh. "I think you're safe. Manny told me about it himself."

"Manny?" Sport choked.

"Didn't you call him Manny when he was down here pouring his heart out to you?"

"I don't think we should be having this conversation," Sport told her in a shaky voice.

Margo reached across the bar and placed her hand over Sport's hand. "Hey, aren't we buddies? Don't you want to help me get this election thing sorted out?"

"Do I have to risk my life sharing state secrets to do it?" came the man's shaky reply.

Margo laughed again. "Okay, I don't care to hear anything about the woman or why she left. I only mentioned this because Morais told me that you and Manny were very close for a time and you might provide some insight into his life and character."

"I was very new on the island back then," Sport nodded, his pupils rolling upward in thought. "I didn't even know the guy was the big cheese until that cab driver fellow told me. He was just another drunk... Well, no, I can't say that because he had already offered to give me this property. I mean I figured out he was some kinda mucky-muck, but I didn't know he was the *big enchilada*."

"Big enchilada." Margo laughed so loud that Moore, Clemmons and the entire crew of the Dexter looked up with big grins and waved her way.

"You know what I mean," Sport replied in a whisper.

"Oh, that's rich," Margo giggled, "Manny the Big Enchilada."

"Quiet, please." Sport cautioned. "I don't need this."

Margo took a moment to compose herself. "Okay, I apologize for any stress I might have caused you. Suffice it to say that I know you know more than you've been letting on. We're in this together, this election thing for Amelia, okay?"

"Sounds like blackmail to me," Sport told her, holding up the vodka bottle to offer her another shot.

"I think I had better switch to beer for the rest of the evening she told Sport with a wink. "Things are getting too weird."

## Chapter Twenty-Two

Margo decided to let it rest and returned to her hotel after a couple beers and a hamburger. Sport seemed to be developing a nervous tick under his left eye.

Opening her laptop in her room, Margo typed copious notes about the day; her interview with Manny, her discussion with the taxi man and Sport's strange reaction to it all.

She then went on line to see if the Internet had a biography of Senhor Souza or any mention of the Supreme Leader's young bride in the sixties. Wikipedia only mentioned that Emmanuel Souza, born October 4th, 1936, was the fifty-fourth Supreme Leader of Santa Nepenthe, a small Portuguese province in the Virgin Islands. They didn't elaborate about personal lives or gossip.

One of those 'ancestry' sites spoke briefly about a common French woman that traveled to Santa Nepenthe and had an affair with the island's ruler which produced two daughters, but didn't give any more details.

By this time Margo was yawning and having trouble focusing on the screen of her computer, so she decided to quit it to bed. What difference did it make anyway? Amelia and Miriam were Manny's daughters and their mother was long gone. Amelia was a very bright girl whatever her lineage and was certainly very capable of ruling Santa Nepenthe; probably more qualified then most of those who went before her.

A string of quiet days passed for Margo. She did some writing in her room, took long walks along the north shore beach and had a few tropical drinks at Sport's in the evenings with supper. Then, on a Friday afternoon she arrived at the beach to find Amelia's big red and blue umbrella parked on the sand near where Morais had dropped her off. The royal daughter was by herself and when she saw Margo, she patted a padded lounger that sat beside her own and lifted a bottle of wine out of a cooler resting between the chairs.

Margo nodded, set her bag down beside the beach chair and reclined upon the lounger. It was a perfect day on the sand, about eighty-five degrees with a light, cooling breeze from the east. Amelia poured a generous slug of red into a large brandy snifter, handed it to Margo and asked, "So have you come up with any ideas for my campaign yet?"

"I was supposed to come up with ideas?" Margo asked, a bit taken aback. "I mean, we haven't even discussed what your campaign is *about* yet."

"It's about getting me elected Supreme Leader," the girl replied, looking at Margo as if she was simple.

"That's a start," Margo told her. "We've established that it's your goal to get elected, but what is your platform? What are you promising the people of Santa Nepenthe?"

"Well, that I'm of royal Souza blood and that I'm therefore the most qualified person for the job." She lifted her glass and took a swallow of the chilled red wine as if to say that the matter was there by settled.

Margo rose halfway out of her chair to face Amelia. "I'm afraid it isn't that simple. If you want to be elected, you'll need to explain to the good voters of this island just what you intend to do for them."

"Well," came the instant reply, "just what we Souza's have *always* done for them. Take care of our people, protect them and keep them safe."

"Not that simple," Margo replied, shaking her head and laying back down in her recliner. "You need a plan to lead your people into the future. Your father gave them telephones, the Internet and television, but there're a lot of other things in this changing world that people need.

"Will you improve the roads; will you build schools to better educate their children? Can you build a hospital on the island and bring in a doctor and some nurses to care for them? Can you promise to install water and sewer lines across the island so all the people can have indoor plumbing? Things like that."

Amelia went very quiet, her eyes closed in thought.

"Well, can you promise your people any of these things? How about a new football stadium that can accommodate more of the population that would like to see the team play?"

"These things would take a lot of money," Amelia sighed, waving the idea away with her hand. "Santa Nepenthe doesn't have a lot of money…"

"So then how can you help them to get more money, have you thought of that?"

"There is only so much money on this island," Amelia stated in a frustrated tone. "This is something I cannot change."

"Maybe not overnight," Margo told her, "but in time. You can promise to bring lots of wonderful new things if the people will work with you and be patient. First, you'll need to bring some commerce to your island. Local shops in the city where they can have access to the kind of things people see on television and now can only buy through the mail using their computers. The citizens of Santa Nepenthe that choose to open shops will make money from the things they buy from other islands and sell here at a profit, then they will pay taxes on their earnings. Taxes can build schools and hospitals, even sports stadiums. I'll bet that any off-islander who would run against you has money to invest in the island."

"The people of my island don't have money to open shops… besides, there are no shops in Cidade Sebastian. Only the butcher, the baker, the army barracks, the hotel and Sport's little bar."

"Then put some of the island men to work building structures for shops. The men who become builders will make more money and pay taxes as well," Margo told her with a broad smile.

"But I already told you," Amelia said, folding her arms across her chest stubbornly. "Santa Nepenthe doesn't *have* much money."

"That's why there are banks in this world," Margo stated emphatically. "You know what a bank is? There are even advanced nations that, when they hear you are holding democratic elections, will offer you free money, what they call foreign aid money, to see that your democracy succeeds."

Amelia shot Margo a questioning eye. "Give free money? They have some of our Gourds to give us?"

"They will give you dollars, *American* dollars, or Euros, both of which are much more valuable than Gourds. But first, you have to… *We* have to come up with a plan.

"I thought you studied political science? Don't you remember learning about international banking or foreign aid to small nations?"

Amelia gave Margo a hurt look. "There was an awful lot to think about. I must have forgotten those things. I know I did have a bank account where I kept money to pay for my books and things. It was money my father somehow put in the bank for me each year."

"Listen, let's set up an appointment to meet with some of your father's ministers, or whatever he calls the men that work for him, and we'll come up with some solid ideas to build for the future of Santa Nepenthe. I'll type it all up in my computer. In the meantime, I'll do some research on the Internet about large countries with aid programs and international banks that make substantial, low-interest loans for developing nations."

Amelia continued to look skeptical, but agreed that she would set up such a meeting for early the next week.

## ☙ Chapter Twenty-Three ☙

On the taxi ride home from the north shore, Margo thought about what she'd just set in motion. She was creating a lot of work for herself when all she wanted to do was write her novel and get back to America to get it published. What did she know about the world of high finance or nations that aided developing countries? She hadn't even worked the business desk at a newspaper since her first job at a small weekly in western Massachusetts where she performed practically all the writing duties.

"You're very quiet today, Ms. Margo," Morais said as they came over the last rise into Cidade Sebastian. "Have you had a falling out with our royal first born?"

"No, no," Margo assured him. "She has just given me a lot to think about."

"Ah, it is about this idea of elections, like America has," the taxi man winked in the mirror. "If we have such elections, it will be a big deal for our island. It will make people have to think and on Santa Nepenthe, we are not used to thinking. We are only used to living day-to-day."

"But you are a thinker," she told the man.

"Yes," Morais smiled. "That is why I drive a taxi cab and make money instead of just eating what I can grow from the earth or catch in a net." He parked the cab on the wharf in front of Sport's place and came around to open Margo's door for her.

Looking up at the man Margo said, "You make money, but what do you spend it on? There isn't much you can do with money on this island." She took the hand he offered and slid out of the old Ford's back seat.

"Well," the old man grinned, "for one thing, I could buy you a drink and then I'll tell you about what else I do with the money I earn."

Seated at the bar with beers in front of them, Morais took a small sip, wiped foam from his lip, and turned to Margo. "Yes, I make money. Not a lot of money each day, but it does add up.

"I have a son who works for Manny, for O Cabeça, as his financial, uh how you would say; finance minister? I guess that would be the word. With the money I made overhauling the old phone system years ago, I sent my son and his sister to New York where my father got them enrolled in a good college, a four year college like where Amelia attended.

"My daughter Catherine, by the way, is O Cabeça's personal secretary. She oversees his serving staff along with running his household."

"I'd never have guessed," Margo exclaimed in amazement.

"Ah yes, but back to my son." Morais took another sip of his beer. "My son, Kennedy is his name, I named him for the great American President. Kennedy oversees the Santa Nepenthe treasury. He collects the taxes and the money from real estate that the off-islanders buy. Then, the dollars he collects, he invests wisely in the world's markets using his computer. I don't understand all of this, but he keeps our island out of debt even though we have little in the way of natural resources."

"You must be very proud." Margo beamed her own drink still untouched.

"Of course I am," the taxi man grinned, "but my son is humble as well. He is not above driving my cab when I take my vacations to America, Portugal and Brazil, which I am able to do sometimes as often as twice a year."

"A world traveler. You meet the most interesting people in the strangest places." And with that, Margo drank some of her beer.

"Thanks to my Kennedy," Morais bragged, "Our Gourd is now strong against other world currencies. Before my son began his work here, our Gourd was practically worthless. Then when we started selling vacation condominiums at Vista Para o Mar, the world markets began to recognize the Gourd."

"Well," Margo mused, "I had never even heard of the Gourd before I landed here. And as your money isn't backed by any kind of reserves, say gold or silver…"

"Ah, but Santa Nepenthe has a little of both, gold and silver I mean. It is buried in our vaults deep beneath the Supreme Leader's palace."

"Gold?" Margo echoed, "silver? Where did you get silver and gold?"

Now Sport had perked up his ears. He came over to where the pair were seated at the bar and poured three shots of his private Estonian vodka, offering two of the small glasses to Morais and Margo. "I thought Santa Nepenthe didn't have any natural resources?" he questioned just before he tossed his own drink down his throat.

The taxi driver took a sip of the proffered vodka and smiled. "These metals are not natural resources. They were brought here many, many years ago. Up until this past century, they rested in this very warehouse that you have made into a bar."

Now the man had Sport and Margo's full attention. They both stared intensely into the man's face.

"It was pirate booty, I think you say. No one remembers if it was from the Spanish or the English. Of course, it must have originally come from Mexico on a Spanish ship, but no one remembers just who brought it here.

"The old legend says that shortly after the English decided our island was worthless and returned it to the Portuguese, a large sailing ship, a privateer, pulled into a cove near where we are now sitting. They were being pursued by another big boat full of pirates, their barquentine had been seriously damaged by cannon fire and most of the crew were dead or dying. The people of Santa Nepenthe scurried and hid from these men, fearful that they might be caught up in a battle that was not their fight.

"A week later two survivors came ashore when their ship finally capsized into the harbor. There was more of a protected cove here at that time I have been told. The rock that had provided shelter fell away in an earthquake two hundred years ago leaving the semi-sheltered harbor we now see."

"I've never heard any of this," Sport exclaimed.

"It is something we Nepenthens learn in our schooling but rarely speak of," the taxi man said with a serious face. He tossed back the rest of his shot, took another sip of beer and continued his story.

"The sunken galleon was resting in shallow mud near the shore. The islanders helped the sailors, who were in very bad shape, to unload their cargo. We built this building where we are now sitting and the other warehouse that houses the army, from the blue ballast bricks in the hold of the wreck, as a safe place to hide the treasure. The two survivors said they would find another ship to take their ill gotten gains away, but would leave a percentage to pay the people of Santa Nepenthe for their help, but these men didn't live that long. One eventually died from an infected slash across his chest made by an enemy cutlass and the other became ill within six months with the fever.

"So the pirate booty and the warehouses became the property of our people, but what use did we have for so much gold and silver. Our island had very little contact with the outside world. Plus, we were afraid to reveal our good fortune to the neighboring islands least they might try to conquer us for this treasure. Our Supreme Leader took charge of the loot in the name of the people and established our first army to guard it."

"That's quite a tale," Margo exclaimed.

"It is what has been passed down to us through the generations," Morais told her finishing his beer and holding his glass out to Sport for a refill.

The next morning, as Margo was finishing up her crab omelet, the pale white man in an even whiter chauffer's uniform and military style cap walked into Sport's bar and took the stool next to hers. Without looking her way, he spoke out of the corner of his mouth.

"You the lady they call Margo?" His accent was pure Hoboken with a hint of Italian. All the cats scurried at the gruff sound of the man's voice.

Margo wiped gravy from her plate with a corn tortilla, popped it in her mouth and washed it down with some of the strong island coffee before acknowledging the man.

"Whose asking?" she replied, looking straight ahead just as the man in white had done and talking out of the side of her face.

The pale man cleared his throat, em'ed and awed a bit then seemed to make a decision. He swiveled his stool to face her, removed his cap and gripped it with both hands in front of his chest. "Mr. Friend sent me to ask if you would be so kind as to accompany me to Vista Para o Mar. Mr. Friend would very much like to speak with you. He has something to show you."

"I'll bet he does," Margo winked. "Question is, do I want to see it?"

"Mr. Friend believes that you do," the man told her. "It concerns the future of this island... and this election that has been proposed."

Sport was standing just down the bar, listening. "If you're not back in two hours, I'll bring the army up there to see what's going on," the barman loudly proclaimed.

"Hey," white suit told Sport with a hurt look. "Al Friend isn't into forcing himself on ladies, or hurting them either. He just wants to have a few words, a little chat. I'll bring her right back here myself. And when I bring her back, you can fill Mr. Friend's growler for me as well."

"Let me look at my calendar," Margo told the man with a stone face. "I'll see if I can work your Mr. Friend in, maybe sometime next week." She turned her head back to the bar and drank some more coffee. Sport was having a hard time keeping a straight face.

The white man placed his cap on the bar and laid a hand lightly on Margo's shoulder. "Mr. Friend is a busy man as well. He says that he will see you today. I'm to drive you out to see him right now."

Margo giggled, "An offer I can't refuse?" She winked at Sport.

The chauffer's face started to turn bright red. He took a series of deep breaths to calm himself and said, "I'm trying to be polite. And I'm just doing what I was told to do. Must we make this difficult?"

"Perhaps Mr. Friend should come here if he wants to speak with one of my customers. I think Margo has other plans for the day."

"Like I said," the very white man replied with pleading in his tone, "Mr. Friend has things he needs to show our lady here. Charts and graphs that display what he plans to do for the people of this piece of rock, even a scale model of the island. It's too large to carry down here in the car. Please, lady. Just give the man an hour or two of your time. How's that gonna hurt you?"

Margo finished her coffee and pushed her empty breakfast plate across the bar before answering. "Okay," she replied. "I suppose just this once. But you better not make a habit of intruding in my life. I am very busy with a number of projects right now." She pointed her two index fingers over the bar at Sport like they were revolvers. "And you have that army ready if I'm gone too long."

## ☞ Chapter Twenty-Five ☜

T he man in white led Margo to a stately old black Mercedes sedan with darkly tinted windows. He opened the right rear door and handed her inside then closed it behind her. They drove in silence through Cidade Sebastian and on into the hills. The man was a sedate and cautious driver, slowing for all the bends in the rough sandy stretch that led to the eastern shore. On approaching the condo development, the man reached up to the car's sun visor and pushed a button. The development's iron gates rolled back before they reached them and, as they entered, a wide garage door was rolling up in one of the farthest buildings inside the development, right at the cliff's edge facing the Atlantic.

Overhead lights came on and the panel rolled down behind them as soon as the Mercedes had cleared it. The man opened Margo's door for her and offered her a hand as she swung her legs out. At the rear of the cavernous space, the man opened another portal and held it for her, motioning Margo inside with a sweep of his hand. She noticed that the man also had another car in his garage, a black BMW convertible, the top-of-the-line model.

Once inside, the white man led her up a short flight of stairs and down a hallway to the left of the huge kitchen where they had entered. Margo noticed that the walls on both sides were covered in framed 8 x 10 photographs. Some were photos of large family gatherings, the men all in dark suits, the ladies in expensive dresses and children sitting calmly in the front. Other frames featured a dark complexioned man with slicked black hair and a deep five-o'clock-shadow posing with various celebrities. A young version of the dark man stood with such celebs as Frank Sinatra, Dean Martin, Al Martino and Tony Bennett. In the more recent snaps, he stood with his arm around people like Celine Dion, Lady Gaga and Jennifer Lopez. In one shot, he stood between Bill and Hillary Clinton, a cigar in his mouth and an arm across each of their shoulders.

The chauffer noticed her slowing to look at the many pictures and chuckled, "Mr. Friend has a lot of friends."

Halfway down the hall, the man stopped before a set of double doors and knocked softly. A loud voice from within shouted, "Come!" and the chauffer opened the door motioning for Margo to proceed him.

The dark man from all the photographs in the hall arose from behind a large desk of polished wood with his hand extended. His wasn't very tall although he had broad shoulders and an expansive waistline. Around a dead stump of cigar he barked, "Come in, Ms. Drelve, come in, sit down, sit." He waved towards a deep and wide white leather couch to the side of his massive desk. "I'm so glad you could spare a few minutes to talk with me, you being a fellow New Yorker and all." His accent, however, sounded more New Jersey than Brooklyn.

"Can I offer you anything?" he asked. "Single malt scotch? Gin? Maybe a coffee?"

Margo smiled. "I'm good, let's just get down to business here. I got things to do."

Al Friend look hurt. "Please, Ms. Drelve. Allow me to be a good host. I could send Johnny out to get lunch for us? Maybe open a bottle of wine? I've got some swell Chianti imported from the old country?"

"Okay, pour me a little wine. Then can we get down to why I'm here?"

The man in the white suit, who Margo assumed must be Johnny, entered with a bottle and two glasses so quickly he must have been eavesdropping on their conversation while he waited out in the hall. He poured a small taste in a glass and held it out for Margo's approval like a professional sommelier. Margo sniffed the liquid, swirled it around in the glass, took a small sip and nodded that it was okay. Only then did the man fill her glass and another for his boss. The beverage served, he gave a quick bow and left the chamber.

Margo tipped her glass toward her host, encouraging him to get on with it. Friend cleared his throat loudly, took another sip of dago red and began. "Word on the street is they might be holding some kind of election on this island."

Margo laughed, "I've heard a rumor like that."

The dark man squinted one eye at her, as though he thought she might be mocking him, but then smiled and continued. "If there should be such an election," he said speculatively, "I plan to throw my hat in the ring." He folded his arms in front of him and dropped them onto the slope of his paunch.

They stared at each other in silence for a minute or two. Finally, Friend broke the staring contest and reached out for his wine. After a long slug of vino, he told her, "I've got some great ideas to bring this little island into the twenty-first century. I think I can give these poor people the better life they deserve as well as put them on the map, so to speak."

"And how are you qualified to lead?" Margo asked.

Friend ignored her impertinence and continued on with his speech. "Most of the men on this rock don't even have real jobs," Friend said with an incredulous look. "They don't know the satisfaction of putting in an honest day's work then returning home to kickback and watch an NFL game. I don't think these people have ever really lived."

"Maybe the people of Santa Nepenthe are content with the simple life they live," Margo countered.

"Oh yeah, sure," Friend barked, his mouth turned down in an exaggerated frown, cigar dangling precariously. "Or maybe they just don't know any better.

"Listen, I've heard the rumors around here. These people, some of them at least, they got televisions in their little mud huts now. They're seeing how the other half lives and they want to get in on it, believe me."

"Okay," Margo mused, "If they elected you as their leader, just how would you improve their lives? Are you going to pour a bunch of money into Santa Nepenthe, build roads and better schools or build better housing for these folks?"

"Better that that," the dark man grinned, "I'm going to help them to help themselves. I'm going to provide a path where they can pull themselves up by their own bootstraps, so to speak, and build their own better life. Here, let me show you something," he said rising out of his chair and waddling around behind his desk. Margo followed, full of curiosity.

In the center of the large room was a table holding an architect's style model of the island. Margo recognized Santa Nepenthe by the outer shape of the construction, but the similarity ended there.

# Friend

The valley where most island farmers grew their crops was flattened, concreted over and flanked by modern glass and steel buildings. Cidade Sebastian looked like some smaller version of Hollywood's Rodeo Drive. Tall structures stood against the sand on both north and south beachfronts and a plastic cruise ship occupied the wharf near Sport's place.

And where was the bar or the other warehouse that served as army headquarters. Both buildings had been replaced by a wide boardwalk.

"Well, what do you think?" Friend asked.

"What is it?" Margo replied, truly baffled.

Friend snapped his fingers and Johnny entered the room, handing him a small aluminum wand that telescoped into a pointer. The dark man tapped his stick on the tower along the northern beach. "This will be Friend's Resort and Casino, a ten story, five-star luxury hotel and gaming area. The tourists we attract will eat this up. It'll have a couple great restaurants, a show lounge, an Olympic-sized swimming pool and lots of tables and slots."

"Tourists will eat this up? What tourists?" Margo quizzed with a pinched face. "We don't get that many tourists here."

"Ah, but we will," the dark man grinned. "They'll fly into Alphonse Ameche International Airport." He tapped his pointer on the flat concreted area in the island's center. "They can stay right here at the Airport Hotel if they like," he continued, tapping his stick on the tall structure to the left of the airport. "The building on the right side will be the terminal. We'll have a subway train under the runways to access the hotel."

Margo's eyes rolled back in her head thinking that all the crazy things she'd heard about this man were true. "I can't believe this," she exclaimed.

"Ah, but there's more," Friend enthused. "By the new and improved Cidade Sebastian, we'll have our second casino, along with the Friend Waterfront Hotel."

"Wait a minute," Margo panicked, "What happens to Sport's bar?"

"We'll move it into the atrium of the Waterfront Hotel," Friend grinned. "A much nicer, more modern bar and it won't cost him a penny. He'll have the exclusive rights to selling alcohol throughout the entire hotel and casino."

"Selling that kind of booze," Margo mused to herself, "the Dexter will have to make daily deliveries."

"The Dexter won't be stopping here anymore," Friend frowned. "Sport can buy his booze from my cousin. Guido has a liquor distributorship in Jersey City. He'll fly all our booze outta Newark, and with the volume discount for all the libations this island will be going through, your friend will be buying at a very handsome discount."

"But there's no fresh water on Santa Nepenthe," Margo sighed, shaking her head. "Will you be flying that in as well?"

"No problem," Friend said taking his cigar out and smiling. "I got another cousin knows a thing or two about desalinating water. The water boiling plant will be around the bend from the port," he told her, pointing out a smaller structure to the east of Cidade Sebastian.

"And who's going to build all this? And staff these businesses?"

"Now there's the beauty of the whole deal," Friend grinned even wider. "We'll put the men of the island to work and pay them decent wages. Construction workers *always* make good bread."

"Do the people of Santa Nepenthe have the necessary skills?" Margo questioned.

"I'll have a few of the guys I know in Boston that work in the trades come down here to train them and oversee the work. I got it all figured. All I have to do is win this election…"

"If there is such an election," Margo put in.

"Well, yeah," Friend agreed, "but I think there will be, and I think I got the thing dicked… er, excuse me, I mean I got it nailed."

## Chapter Twenty-Six

"**Y**ou've been meeting with Alphonse Friend," Amelia cried with a hurt look. "I thought you were helping me?"

"But I *am* helping you," Margo pleaded. "I'm letting you know what he's planning, his strategy for trying to win over the people of Santa Nepenthe. Besides, he practically kidnapped me, just ask Sport. He sent that albino henchman of his to fetch me and the man wouldn't take 'no' for an answer."

Margo had telephoned Amelia as soon as Johnny had returned her to Sport's bar, telling the woman that they needed to get together immediately and that the senior Souza should attend their meeting as well, but Amelia told her that the Supreme Leader was playing bridge this afternoon with some of his top staffers and couldn't be disturbed. Amelia suggested that Margo have Morais bring her to the north beach once more.

"Put Sport on the line," the royal daughter suggested. "I'll ask him to prepare a picnic hamper for us and we'll eat while we talk. It's almost lunch time and I'm simply starving."

"Amelia," Margo scolded. "This is serious business. That Friend guy is insane and his plans are almost crazy enough to get him elected."

"We'll talk all about it shortly," Amelia said. "Now let me talk to Sport. Do you like chicken salad sandwiches?"

When the barman had replaced the telephone receiver back in its cradle, Margo asked, "Do you have some more of that special vodka under the bar? I think I'll need a couple strong belts of liquid lunch before I can face a picnic with that daft Souza woman."

Sport had the bottle out and was turned to fetch clean shot glasses before Margo had finished speaking. The man was grinning at her. "Too bad you don't have that scale model to show her. I'm surprised there isn't a golf course laid out somewhere on Friend's island plan."

"Oh, that's coming," Margo barked. "He said that's in his five year plan but he wants to get the airport and casinos up, running and turning a profit before he starts laying out his eighteen holes. Proper golf links might require a second desalination plant to keep everything green and lovely."

The island taxi had arrived just as Sport was putting a pot of potato salad into the picnic basket with the sandwiches. Morais carried the basket out and placed it into the trunk of the old Ford, then he opened the front passenger door. "We are drinking buddies now, Ms. Margo." He'd said, "Would you like to sit up front with me? If you like, you can call me Maynard."

"Why thank you, Maynard. And you may call me Margo."

And now, sitting on a red and blue beach chair with the royal seagull and gourd crest embossed into the fabric, before a small portable table, Margo was trying to talk sense to Amelia while the nervous girl stuffed chicken salad into her face. Margo's sandwich sat on the table untouched along with her glass of wine. "All the rumors are true. I saw the plans for the airport, hotels and the casinos. These things are very real. You'd just better hope the people have enough faith in your traditions," she told the royal daughter. "Because Friend intends to literally bribe his way to victory while he totally changes the way people here have lived for so many hundred years. He'll have enough good paying jobs for every Nepenthen that wants to work. And he'll be bringing in stores and shops where the locals can spend their money on the things they've only seen on the Internet or dreamed of."

"He won't be using our treasury to build these big dreams," Amelia said around a mouthful of potato salad. "Kennedy would never permit such a thing." She nodded her head for emphasis. "And Kennedy has to co-sign for every denaré our government spends."

"This friend character just may have money of his own to invest," Margo told the girl. "He would certainly stand to make a fortune off such investments. And if he doesn't have enough of his own, the show he's prepared would be pretty enticing to any off-island investors, individuals or big banks. He plans to turn your island into a money making machine."

"But from what you've told me, this man wants to change our island forever. It just won't be Santa Nepenthe anymore. I don't think our people would want to live in such a place…"

"I wouldn't be so sure," Margo cautioned. "So don't you think we should arrange an audience with your father to let him know about this?"

"I'll mention it to him," Amelia said as she took a big swallow of wine to wash down her lunch. "Aren't you hungry? You haven't even touched your food."

"Amelia, I'm worried. I'm worried that you aren't taking this election business seriously and I'm concerned that this man, Friend, is going to trash one of the last remaining natural islands in the Caribbean. Once the man makes changes like this, Santa Nepenthe will never be able to go back to what it once was. Even if everyone hates what it becomes. Once you let the genie out of the bottle..."

"So, have you found me some money that I can use to build roads and schools once I'm elected Supreme Leader?" Amelia asked, changing the subject. She swirled her wine glass around, looked into the liquid and then took another swallow before returning her eyes to Margo.

"I don't think you've heard a word I've said." Margo stamped her foot in the sand for emphasis. "You are up against a man, possibly a criminal, who wants to take over your island for his own *personal* gain. Sure, he's willing to spread some money around to the population. What has he got to lose? He might even pay a small percent of his profits in tax.

"I'm sure he'll build new roads, but they won't be for the locals. He'll build highways to ferry his customers between the airport and his casinos. I doubt if the man truly cares one little bit for any of the people of this island. Mark my words, it will be all about him."

"Well, I guess it's something to think about," Amelia told her with an air of disinterest. "But I'm going to be the next Supreme Leader. Our people love my family. They've always loved and respected the Souzas on Santa Nepenthe."

Stifling a scream, Margo downed her glass of wine in one go, poured more from the bottle and slammed that down as well, then she took off down the beach at a quick march. She didn't even look back at the royal daughter. How long would she have to wait before that damn taxi returned?

## Chapter Twenty-Seven

"**B**ut this woman is supposed to have an *education*," Margo shouted at Sport. "Dual degrees. Economics and Political Science, I think she said. And still she's clueless."

"A person can learn all about a subject," Sport ventured, "but if they don't have any practical application in their own life, it becomes purely academic. Knowledge that you don't put to everyday use… I think they say you might retain about three-percent of it if you're lucky.

"Does Amelia read? Or does she keep up on any of what she's learned? Is she interested in politics in or around the outside world?"

"I don't know any of this," Margo lamented. "I hardly know the woman at all. The only thing I could say from what I've seen of her is that she has some sort of princess complex. She's obsessed with following in her father's footsteps."

"And Emmanuel Souza has no formal education whatsoever." Sport laughed, "Nor did any of the *O Cabeças* before him, so she's just as qualified as anyone else in this island's history."

"None of those before her had to face a popular election either," Margo reminded the bar man. "This is a whole new page in history and someone needs to knock her upside the head to make her aware of that."

Sport laughed at this image. "So I guess that must be your call-ing, Marg. Are you up to the challenge?"

"No, I am damn well not!" Margo shouted, holding out her empty shot glass. Sport refilled it from the vodka bottle under the counter, his own private stock.

Margo tossed back the full shot of liquor then said, "But, on the other hand I'm not ready to see some New Jersey hoodlum buy an entire unspoiled island to turn it into a cash cow for himself and his buddies. Did I tell you he plans to cancel the Dexter's contract and fly all the island's supplies in by air? He says you'll have to buy all your booze from some cousin of his in Jersey City."

"I'll deal with that if and when it happens," Sport told her pour-ing himself a shot. "Personally, I kinda like Captain Moore and his boys. I'd be sorry to see them go... And the cash they spend in here."

Margo slept late the next morning. When she awoke she went next door to the bakery and bought a bag of sweet pastries to go with her coffee. She carried everything out to the hotel's terrace overlooking the harbor, set out her coffee and breakfast next to her computer and got right down to work on her novel, pushing island problems and politics to the rear of her consciousness.

She was making excellent progress at refining two or three of her protagonists when Ms. Hix came out holding a telephone on a very long chord. "Mr. Sport for you," she purred holding out the receiver.

"Margo," the journalist barked, placing the instrument in the crook of her shoulder as she continued to type with the fingers of one hand.

"You alright, kid?" Sport queried. "I was worried when you didn't show up here for something to eat."

"I'm fine, Sport. I just decided to get some serious writing done this morning, without a lot of interruptions. I've been doing too much for everyone else lately and not enough for myself. Maybe I'll stop by later…"

"Okay," Sport told her, "just call if you need me."

Margo passed the phone back to Ms. Hix without another word, ignoring the hand the girl held out for a tip, and returning to her story. It took her a moment to retrieve a thought she'd had just before the phone call had diverted her attention.

Soon the story was back on track and Margo's fingers were flying over the keypad, ideas coming almost faster than she could type. That's when Ms. Hix appeared again with her improvised mobile telephone.

"Some guy calls himself Johnny wants to talk to you," she told Margo, then popped a pink bubble-gum bubble that caught the tip of her nose. As Margo grabbed the handset once more, Ms. Hix peeled gum from her nose.

"Yeah," Margo said without feeling. Friend's little albino henchman was the last person on the island, or on earth for that matter, that she wanted to talk to.

"I looked for you at that waterfront bar," came the Jersey accent through the receiver. "But I guess you wasn't there."

"No, I wasn't there," Margo parroted. "And I'm not going there or anywhere else right now, so what do you need?"

"Mr. Friend, he wants to know what you think of his plans for the island, like, now that you've had some time to sleep on it."

"I've been sleeping on 'the island,' as you put it for some four months now, and sleeping just fine, now if you'll excuse me…"

"No, wait lady, please. Mr. Friend wants to know what you think…"

"Of his ideas," the lady finished his sentence for him. "Yeah I know. You can tell him I haven't given his big money plan another thought. I think it's a terrible idea now, just like when he first showed it to me. And I'm not going anywhere today, so don't come by to see me or to fetch me. I've got plenty of work on my plate."

"Work like helping these Souza people?" the man asked with some irritation.

"Work like I'm writing a book. That's what I came to Santa Nepenthe to do, to find peace and quiet to write my book. And assho… uh, *people* like you keep bothering me, keeping me from my project." She abruptly hung up the telephone and shoved it into Ms. Hix arms, giving her a dirty look, then thinking better of it she said, "I'm sorry, Ms. Hix. It's not your fault, but please, the next time that thing rings, tell them I died or left the island or something, **please!**"

The desk girl nodded understanding as she peeled more pink sticky stuff from her nose. "Now where was I?" Margo mumbled to herself returning her gaze to her screen. She had to scroll up a page or two to refresh her thoughts, but the story started coming together for her again without too much lost time. She reread a particularly meaty sentence, feeling proud of herself for the intricate wording she had woven, reached for another sugary bun that looked something like an apple fritter and washing it down with the last of her coffee.

Margo thought about going to her room to make a fresh espresso, but decided she would complete the current chapter as it seemed to be going so well. Her New York detective was trapped in a corner of a cheap hotel room on the twelfth floor without his weapon. What could he use to defend himself? A makeshift knife or...

Her musings were shaken again, this time by a tap on her shoulder. She'd been so engrossed in her plot that Margo hadn't even heard Ms. Hix's footfalls crossing the red clay times.

"Sorry to bother you again, Ms. Margo," the girl whined. "But it's Amelia Souza. I *knew* you'd want to take a call from one of the royal family."

Margo's eyes shot daggers at the woman, but she took the proffered telephone. "Amelia, I'm rather busy right now."

"Busy checking on money grants for me?" the royal daughter inquired with enthusiasm.

"Busy doing what I came to this island to do," Margo answered in an abrupt tone. "I'm working on my novel. By the way, have you discussed what we talked about the other day, about Friend's big plans for Santa Nepenthe, with your father?"

"I started to," Amelia said hesitantly, "but he got very upset. Antonio, one of his servants, had to bring father one of his pills to calm him down. I'm not sure if I should try to tell him again."

"Amelia," Margo barked sternly, "you must tell him, or, better than that, set up a meeting between me and your father. And you should be there as well, and Kennedy. Kennedy needs to be in on this too.

"And thinking about it, Kennedy would be a much better person than me to help you find foreign aid grants or sympathetic banks. He works with financial things like this every day. I'm just an investigative journalist trying to write a saleable novel."

Amelia sounded hurt. "But I thought we were friends?" she whimpered.

"Amelia, we are friends and, believe me I'd like to help you, but there are much more qualified people all around you. Let's just stay friends. I'm afraid that if I say or do too much with your campaign to rule the island, we won't be friends for long." Margo realized that her voice had been steadily increasing in volume. She made a point of softening her pitch to say, "We'll get together for a talk and a glass of wine soon. And we need to arrange that meeting with your father and Kennedy," she emphasized.

"Okay, bye Margo," came across the line followed by an upset sniffle and then the phone went dead.

Margo thrust the instrument back at Ms. Hix mumbling, "Oh, I give up." When Ms. Hix had left the patio, Margo packed up her things and headed up to her room. She rinsed out her coffee cup, checked her hair in the mirror and headed down the hill to the wharf side.

## Chapter Twenty-Eight

Arriving at the bar, Margo found First Officer Clemmons seated on her usual stool in such a deep conversation with Sport that neither noticed her entrance into the room. She parked herself on the next seat over and cleared her throat which brought both men's heads around.

"We were just talking about you," Clemmons offered. "Sport tells me you've heard some rumor about an airport here putting my little Dexter tub out of business." Margo noticed there were two empty shot glasses on the bar. She guessed that the ship's first officer had been upset enough with the news, even if it wasn't an immediate threat, that they'd been knocking back Sport's special vodka to cope with it.

"I don't know about putting you out of business," Margo replied, "but Mr. Friend says that if he were to rule Santa Nepenthe, he'd eliminate your trips to this island…"

"Putting us out of business," continued Clemmons. "Santa Nepenthe is our bread-and-butter client, you might say. It's the only steady run we can count on. Besides our trips between Puerto Rico and here, we might get the odd run to some island that's short of something and can't get their regular supplier, or maybe we'd make the odd unscheduled delivery of some large item somewhere, but nothing that could support us as a viable carrier. Without our monthly check from old Souza, we might as well curl up and die."

Margo looked at Sport for confirmation. "How much do you pay the Dexter for shipping the booze and food they bring you?"

Sport returned a sheepish look. "The island takes care of that," he explained. "Part of the deal Emmanuel Souza offered me when I landed here. I pay Kennedy, Souza's accountant, for the actual items I use but the government pays Captain Moore a set fee each month for bringing my stuff along with supplies for the palace, the condo owners at Vista Para o Mar and other businesses. They also carry the mail between here and the outside world."

"And if Santa Nepenthe had an airport where supplies and mail could come by air?" Margo asked.

"It would probably cost a little more," Sport replied thoughtfully. "And there are things that I don't think they could fly in, like the fifty-five gallons of gas we use every month."

"If Friend brings in cars for the islanders, or busses for tourists," Margo surmised, "this island will need a lot more than fifty-five gallons of gas at a shot. They'll probably need that much two or three times a day."

First Officer Clemmons laughed. "We couldn't bring that much gas here if we wanted. Moore would have to buy a tanker ship. And none of us on the crew are qualified to run a tanker. The fuel we bring here now is prepackaged in fifty-five gallon drums, old oil drums." Clemmons eyed the empty glass in front of him.

"Need one more shot?" Sport asked. The sailor nodded in the affirmative.

Sport tilted his head toward Margo. "Why not?" she said with a shrug. "My day isn't going all that well anyway. I mean my day *was* going along pretty super until everybody in the world decided to interrupt what I was doing."

Sport gave her a sympathetic look to which Margo spit back at him, "You started it, calling to check on me."

Sport quickly filled a shot glass right to the brim and slid it in front of the woman. "Hey, I was just concerned, that's all."

Margo tossed back her shot, shook her head rapidly a few times and then gave Sport a smile. "Sorry," she apologized. "Nothing personal, I had just decided this would be a really productive day on my book and that I was going to put myself one-hundred-percent into creating and nothing else. After you called, that albino freak that works for Friend telephoned wanting to know if I was properly impressed with that mobster's plans to trash the island. I think he had in mind to kidnap me for another brain-washing session at his master's place…"

"He was in here looking for you," Sport confessed. "I told him I didn't know where you were."

"Thanks for that, but he found me anyway. And that wasn't the end of it. Princess Amelia rang not long after Johnny wanting more help with her campaign. It just isn't my day."

"You're working for the Souza family's election now?" Clemmons asked.

"Not if I can help it," Margo barked. "I tried to give that Amelia girl some advice, but she's as thick as a pair of two-by-fours. I'm afraid if I offer the slightest bit of help that girl will fasten herself to me like a leach and try to suck me dry."

As Margo was saying this, Captain Moore came through the wide double warehouse doors with the remainder of the Dexter's crew. "I guess I had better give him the news," Clemmons said sotto voce.

"The rumor, you mean," Sport laughed. "If we're lucky it will never really be news. But, yeah, you'd better let him know. Maybe Moore can put together some kind of alternate plan."

## Chapter Twenty-Nine

Two days later, Maynard Morais came into Sport's place to tell Margo that the Supreme Leader and Kennedy would see her in two hours.

"I told them you might need some time to prepare your notes. And be forewarned that Amelia is going a bit koo-koo over all this. She's afraid that you might say something that would leave her father to question if she's up to the job of following in his footsteps."

Margo just rolled her eyes at which Morais laughed. "I know how you feel," he told her, "but what choices do we have? I'm sure Manny wasn't really up to the job when his father, Abraham, died all those years ago, but Manny's done a fine job thanks to others in the government who were able to set him on a steady course. Maybe a world war breaking out just before his father assumed leadership duties gave Abraham some wisdom that helped mature Manny into his leadership role, I couldn't say, but I think he's done well.

"Guidance from you and your children sure didn't hurt anything," Sport put in leaning across the bar. So do you have some other clients to chauffeur around the island before you escort Ms. Margo to the palace or would you have time for a spot of lunch?"

"Lunch, by all means," the taxi man grinned. "Margo, will you join me?"

Margo looked up from her laptop, "That would be nice," she told the man. "What's on the menu today, Sport?"

"One of the locals just brought me a few pounds of Mahi-Mahi," Sport told her. "It's tender and it's fresh, served on a bed of coconut rice and peas. Or I could make up some poor boy sandwiches if you're not that hungry?"

"We are hungry, are we not, Margo?" Morais grinned, "And thirsty as well. How about we start with a couple draught beers?"

The two sipped at their suds while Sport went back to the kitchen to prepare their meal. "So," Margo began, "did I tell you about my trip to Friend's place?"

"I never took you to the condos," Morais said with knitted brows. "You went to see this man Friend?"

"Believe me, it wasn't by choice," the lady told him. "The man sent some albino heavy in a white suit here to kidnap me. This little hood, Johnny is what Friend called him, he dragged me over to Vista Para o Mar and escorted me to Friend's office where that sleazy man had a tabletop model of Santa Nepenthe." She explained about the airport, the hotels, casinos and the desalinating plant. "And the man plans to move Sport's bar into one of his hotels and tear down all the historic buildings of Cidade Sebastian," she concluded. "The people of this island might as well be packed up and moved to Miami Beach."

"A project like this could take decades," the taxi man laughed. "And cost billions of dollars. I hope the people of Santa Nepenthe are smart enough to realize that they probably won't see any of this in their lifetime."

"But Friend says this is all in his five-year plan. He says he already has the money and he wants to have all this built and bringing in more money in five years or less."

"And he plans on using islanders for labor? The man obviously doesn't know much about the character of Nepenthens. The men of our island may *say* they want jobs, but only when the fish aren't biting and the weather isn't perfect. These are not hard workers, and I think our Friend will learn this quickly should he win the vote."

Margo looked skeptical. "I don't know. The man seems pretty sure of himself."

## Chapter Thirty

Emmanuel Souza had ordered mountains of pastries and plenty of coffee from the Cidade Sebastian Bakery for their meeting. Maynard Morais delivered Margo to the palace sharply at ten a.m. and two of the soldiers, all smiles this time, handed her from the taxi, then opened the door of the opulent building for her.

The meeting was held in a small conference room upstairs. Kennedy was seated to Manny Souza's left at the head of the table with his laptop to one side. Miriam and Amelia were to the Supreme Leader's right, Amelia having a yellow legal pad and several Bic pens before her to take notes. Morais' daughter, Catherine, stood at the back of the hall with two maids who came forth to pour coffee and offer plates for the goodies.

Both the men stood when Margo entered the room and remained standing until one of the palace guards had pulled a chair out for her and, when she sat, pushed her chair into the table.

"Daddy," Amelia purred, "Have you met Margo? She's from New York and she's been helping me with my campaigning.

"I have had the pleasure," Emmanuel Souza grinned, showing two rows of teeth so perfect that Margo wondered if they might be caps. "Welcome to my humble, ah, digs. I am so happy you chose to come to our island and that you have become a friend to my wonderful daughters. Please, help yourself to some Danish.

"I understand that you might have some insight into the matter of our promised election? You have spoken with this man, Friend, who has decided to run against my daughter for the office I have held all these years."

"I didn't meet with the man by choice," Margo shuddered. "Actually I took an instant dislike to the man."

"And why is this," Manny Souza asked. "I've not met the man myself, only heard about him."

"He's just, uh, creepy," Margo replied. "You understand creepy?"

The O Cabeça laughed loudly. "Yes, I know this expression. Others have said similar things of this man. So what did you learn on this visit with him?"

"Well, for one thing," Margo told the Supreme Leader, "he plans to spoil your beautiful island, to take away much of its charm. He wants to build hotels and gambling halls here to attract tourists..."

"A few tourists might not be a bad thing..." Manny Souza pondered.

"Not a few tourists," Margo stated emphatically. "He wants to bring in *hundreds* of tourists, more tourists then you have native islanders. He plans to build an airport large enough to land the biggest jet airplanes in the world right in the middle of your richest farming lands. I've seen his models of this."

"Do you think he might settle for a better dock at Cidade Sebastian so tourists can just come here by boat?"

Kennedy raised his head and commented, "I think this man is wishing to make lots of money from our island. The kind of money he wants would require more tourists than could be brought here by small boats or even cruise ships."

Margo was nodding her head up and down. "Kennedy's right. When I was at Friend's condo, he had a big model of the island. His mock-up of Santa Nepenthe had ten story tall hotels on both the north and south coasts, as well as another large hotel in the island's center by his airport."

Manny Souza laughed. "And he'd better warn these people that they must bring their own water. We have no water here for such a number of tourists."

"He also plans to build a plant that will boil sea water and make it drinkable."

The Supreme Leader's face clouded over. "He is serious then. He really intends to build all these things? They would not just be empty politician's promises to the people."

"He's dead serious," Margo told the man. "His political promise to your people is that all this tourist stuff will provide them with good paying jobs so that they can buy all the things they have seen on the Internet. Things like fast cars, computer games and kitchen appliances."

"Fast cars would not be able to go so fast on our roads, believe me," Kennedy put in.

"Well, Friend also plans to build highways all over Santa Nepenthe, concrete highways with four lanes for fast traffic."

Manny Souza took a deep breath, held it for a few seconds and then exhaled. "I don't like the sound of all this. When you say good paying jobs..."

"He plans to hire the men of your island, first to build the airport and then to construct the hotels and casinos. Later, when everything is up and operating, he'll have jobs for the women of Santa Nepenthe as hotel maids and waitresses."

"I will have to give this much thought," the old man said in a velvet voice, "Now, what about the campaign for my daughter, Amelia."

"I've made some suggestions," Margo told him. "I think Amelia should promise to build more schools; a high school where your people can learn about the world outside, and a hospital, things that will serve the people rather than pour wealth into some off-islander's pocket. Paving the roads you have would be good as well, maybe renovate the existing hotel to make it more welcoming, with a restaurant where guests can take meals..."

"All this would be good," old Souza said, "but we are not a rich island."

Kennedy perked up at this, "Manny? Ms. Drelve has given us some good thoughts about that. She suggested that Amelia might check about borrowing seed money to help us. She also mentioned that many large nations like America sometimes give away money they call foreign aid to help nations that hold democratic elections. I've been doing some research on these things. Our own bank is reviewing the business that we've given them in the years since the war. They are right now trying to decide just how much money they might be willing to loan to us that we might build these schools, roads and a hospital."

Manny Souza sat back in his plush leather chair, his face spreading into a satisfied grin.

"I haven't heard back from America yet," Kennedy continued. "As soon as America and the banks give me an answer, I will sit down with Amelia and we will see just how much we can promise our people if your daughter becomes the Supreme Leader."

## ✾ Chapter Thirty-One ✾

"Is there any more I should know about this election business?" Old Souza asked. "It sounds like my Amelia and Senhor Kennedy have things well in hand."

"Ah, well, Manny, one more thing. I'd like to get your blessing to spend some of our treasury on signs and posters asking the people to vote for Amelia." Kennedy looked nervously at the old man. "Not a lot of money, you understand, sir. But we must order these items from off island. From someplace in America called Vista Print. We don't have a printing press capable of producing such things."

Manny Souza's brow creased in thought. He took a drink from his coffee cup and nibbled on a prune-flavored sweet roll. The old man pushed the last of the pastry into his face, took out a white silk handkerchief to dust crumbs from his lips and, with a nod, said, "I think that will be in order. Is there anything else?"

"Yes, there is," Margo piped up. "Are you aware that this Friend character is a criminal? He's suspected of being part of an organized crime ring in America, a gangster. I researched the man on the Internet after I met with him in his condo. Police records in New Jersey, that's in America, say that Friend isn't even his real name. The man was born Alphonse Ameche. He calls himself A. Friend to avoid the police."

Manny Souza and Kennedy Morais looked at each other in surprise. "And has this man, Friend or Ameche, whatever his name is, has he done time in an American jail or prison?"

"He's seems to be very clever," Margo told them. "And he has good lawyers. No one has ever been able to prove that he's committed any crimes, but he's suspected of a long list of bad deeds."

Souza gave Kennedy a long look, then turned his head to Margo. "Friend hasn't broken any laws on my island. He hasn't shown any suspicious behavior here, has he Kennedy?"

"No sir," came the reply. "He keeps to himself and doesn't cause any trouble. I don't know if we can call him a model citizen, but he *does* pay his taxes on time. In fact, he pays twice a year, six months in advance. And, although I've never seen him at a match, he donates money each year to support our football club. Last year, in fact, he bought the entire team new uniforms."

The O Cabeça nodded again. "I can't accuse a man who has shown no leanings toward bad behavior on my island. On Santa Nepenthe, like in America, a man must be assumed to be innocent until he is proven guilty. Perhaps our Senhor Friend has turned over a new leaf, is that how you say it?"

"I strongly doubt that," Margo said, folding her arms across her chest.

"I will have my army people keep an eye on him," old Souza said. "Now, if you will excuse me, I have island business to which I must attend."

After the O Cabeça exited the room, Amelia turned to Margo. "Do you think I should be worried that this man, Friend, might not play fair in the elections? He wouldn't murder me just to win, would he?"

"I would count on him trying unfair tactics in order to beat you, but I doubt if he would stoop to murder. Santa Nepenthe is a small island and I don't think you have smart lawyers here that could protect him. If Friend were to kill someone here, no one would ever let him rule the island."

"Would you like to go to the beach with my sister and me?" Amelia asked. "It's another perfect day out there. I've got a few bottles of wine for us."

"Maybe another day," Margo told the royal daughter. "I'm a little behind in my writing right now. I really should be getting back to the hotel."

"Maybe Miriam and I could come by Sport's place this evening and buy you dinner?"

"That would be lovely," Margo laughed, "But not to talk politics. I want to relax in the evening when I'm through working."

## ☙ Chapter Thirty-Two ☙

**M**argo was sitting on the bench in front of Sports, her laptop balanced on her knees, editing what she'd written over the past few weeks while enjoying the sunshine when Morais' old Ford pulled up alongside of her.

"Hey Margo, are you busy right now?" he asked in greeting.

"Depends on what you have in mind," Margo chuckled with a little leer.

"The Santa Nepenthe Panthers are playing a home game this afternoon against Santiago de Cuba. It should be quite fun and interesting too."

"Well, I've never been much of a sports fan," Margo said hesitatingly, "Maybe some other time."

Maynard Morais got out of his car and came to sit on the bench next to her. "Whether you enjoy football or not, I think you'll enjoy this experience. It will give you the chance to see how the other half of this island lives. Give you some strong insight into our culture."

"I'm supposed to be having dinner here with the royal sisters," Margo stated. "Can you have me back here before six?"

Morais laughed loudly, "Of course, my girl. The match starts at two, so it will all be over by around four o'clock. Have you even seen our football stadium? It's just behind the cathedral, but I don't recall pointing it out to you when I gave you that island tour so many months ago. I was suspicious of you... I mean before I got to know you, you were just another off-islander."

Margo gave him a questioning look. Was everyone here suspicious of the outside world?

"You can sit up front with me because I have a couple other fares headed that way."

Margo packed up her laptop and put her large purse in the trunk of the vehicle. She then slid through the passenger door of the Ford and they took off up the main road through town.

Morais took a side road halfway up the hill that Margo hadn't noticed before. He drove about two miles over very rough gravel until they came to a rambling two-story shack that looked like it was constructed of palm leaves lashed around a perfect square of coconut trees. Two men sat in rickety chairs on the dirt porch of the structure. They stood and waved when they saw the taxi approaching. As the cab pulled abreast of their house, the men came to the driver's window and passed through a handful of Gourd notes, then they grabbed the rear door handle and let themselves into the car.

Morais half turned in his seat. "João, Claus, I want you to meet Margo. Margo is from New York and she's down here writing a book. Margo, these are my friends João and Claus. Margo has never seen the Panthers play before."

"Oh, senhora, you are in for a treat!" Claus erupted. "And with this match especially." "Santiago is one of the toughest teams we've played, but we are ready for them," João added.

The taxi man put the car in gear and they back tracked to the main road where they turned left and continued up the rise. Just short of the cathedral, Morais turned onto another road that was little more than dual tracks worn into the scrub. Margo made the observation to herself that, while so much of Santa Nepenthe looked like scruffy, barren desert, anywhere that there was a substantial low spot in the ground where water could pool and sink in, there would be a thick patches of jungle growth.

They followed this rutted trail for five miles or more, passing a number of shack-like structures, almost to the island's western edge where they came upon a hovel hammered together from weathered packing crates. On some of the slats, Margo could make out a very faded stamp that said 'Property of US Navy.'

Morais tooted his horn and a wizened old figure came slowly forth leaning on a homemade cane of some dark wood. "Hey, Maynard," he shouted as he approach the car's rear door. He slid in next to João and Claus asking, "Who's the fine looking young lady? You're not from around here, missy or I would have noticed you before." He extended a handful of cash over the seat to the driver.

Margo turned in her seat and smiled at the man.

"Name's Reggie," he told her and offered a hand over the seat to shake, but when Margo extended her own, Reggie took it in his own, leaned over and kissed it. Then he leaned back and shouted, "On to the coliseum!"

Behind the cathedral, they came upon a large patch of grass greener than anything Margo had seen on Santa Nepenthe, even greener then the plantings around Vista Para o Mar. On two sides, sets of aging bleachers paralleled the grass, possibly more seventy-year-old war surplus?

And people. She'd never seen so many people in all her months on Santa Nepenthe. Many were dressed in obviously homemade clothes, but a few were smartly dressed in dazzling white shorts or Levi jeans and tropical design sport shirts. As they headed for their seats, Margo asked, "Where do some of these islanders get the fancy apparel. Does it all come from the Internet?"

Morais laughed again as they parked their bottoms on the aged and weathered wood, "You're looking at our football club, Margo, some of the most revered and important people on the island. When our team plays away games, on St Thomas, Cuba, Martinique or wherever, they always bring home gifts for their friends. Tommy Bahama shorts are popular right now. The well dressed young men and women you see are friends and family to our team players. Would you care for a beer?"

"We're a long way from Sport's place," she replied quickly, then noticed a handsome young mahogany-toned man in Khaki Cabela's shorts and what looked like a genuine Reyn Spooner Hawaiian shirt dragging a large blue Igloo cooler up the steps toward them. Morais held out some Gourd notes and the man opened the cold box to reveal dozens of bottles of Jamaican Red Stripe beer well packed in the ice. He popped the top on one with an old-fashioned church key that hung from a chain on his belt, handed it to Margo then opened the other for Morais, shouting a hearty "T'anks, Captain," as he moved along.

"Jeremy," the taxi man explained. "He somehow ended up on the Panther's yacht after a match in Ocho Rios and decided to stay here. His uncle in Jamaica sends us over a dozen cases of beer on the boat every time we play there.

Then the two teams came trotting out onto the field, all looking very serious. The Panthers were in scarlet and navy blue uniforms, the island's colors. The Cuban players wore blue and white. The team members walked down the line shaking hands with their rivals and then a bell sounded and they got in position for the kick-off.

As the two teams passed and dribble the ball, Maynard Morais explained to Margo how if Santa Nepenthe had a true middle class, it included these footballers as well as himself and the island's few shopkeepers. He pointed to a small, newer appearing building at the far end of the field.

"That's the team store," he told her. "Fans can buy official jerseys with their favorite player's number, tee-shirts, or soccer balls or even some historic items."

"Historic?" Margo questioned, "Historic like how?"

"Well, like the jersey a player wore when he scored two goals in one game, things like that." Morais smiled. "It may not sound like much to you, but these people take their football very seriously."

"Oh, I think I get it. The Sport's Editor of our newspaper collects some pretty weird stuff that he calls 'memorabilia, like some NFL players old jockstrap."

## Chapter Thirty-Three

As the game went on, Margo and Morais had a couple more Jamaican beers and she found she was quite enjoying herself. At one point, a thin man in a Panther jersey came rushing forward into a tangle of Cuban players near the Santa Nepenthe goal, each man doing his best to keep passing the ball out of their opponent's reach. The Panther man came up from behind and kicked the ball out from under one of the Cubans who was attempting a dribble toward the back field. The ball sailed smoothly past the goalie and Morais was on his feet shouting praises.

Margo was surprised by this outburst from a man she'd so far found rather subdued, but she didn't say anything. When the men at the top of the opposite stand posted the score, Santa Nepenthe two, Cuba nil, he turned to explain.

"That's my grandson, Jacob. What a fine boy, did you see how he outfoxed that Cuban guard?"

"I didn't know you had a grandson," said Margo.

"Catherine's boy," the taxi man beamed. "When she went to school in New York, she brought Jake back with her. Alas no father followed them home. But Catherine has managed well. Working in the palace has been a big help. Jacob grew up alongside Amelia and Miriam, and that crazy Junior too, but I don't think he counts for much."

"And that's why you wanted me to see the game," Margo chuckled. "Well, you should be very proud. And I'm enjoying this, even though I don't quite understand it all.

Before the game was over, Jacob had scored again, this time bobbing and zigzagging through tight opposition, head butting the ball high into the air, then running forward, his kick catching the orb on its decent and slamming it past the surprised goalie who had been seemingly mesmerized by young Jacob's weasel like movements.

Morais asked if Margo she would like to take a look at the team store after the game was over and she said, "Why not?" They strolled down the sidelines as happy players poured Champagne over each other's heads. Where did they get the Champagne on Santa Nepenthe, she wondered? Yes, she was getting some new insight into what she'd thought of as a quiet and sleepy little atoll. The taxi man stopped briefly to shake his son's hand then give him a big hug and finished up rubbing his knuckles on the man's head with a laugh.

The team store was doing a great business with customers five deep at the register waiting to pay for their purchases. Margo checked the displays. Levi jeans were piled on a card table; the overhead sign said two-hundred Gourds a pair. Could that be right? She tried to do the math in her head but simply ended up accepting that this must be almost three times what you'd pay at Macy's. Then there was a jersey that, according to the plaque beneath it, had been worn by Tom Costa in two different games where he'd scored multiple goals to beat a scoreless opposition. Who on this island could afford to pay three-hundred Gourd just for an old souvenir of someone else's previously worn clothing?

The taxi's three passengers were waiting by the old Ford when they returned to the parking area behind the cathedral. All of them looked like they'd enjoyed a few beers. Of course they were in great spirits after seeing their team defeat a formidable enemy. On the road heading home, the men sang something over-and-over in Portuguese, the only word Margo recognized in it was 'Panthers.'

When they reached old Reggie's house of crates, he took her hand and kissed it again, praising Morais for his taste in woman as though Margo was Maynard's mistress or something.

As the cab reached their door, Claus and João each slapped the back of the driver's seat. "Same again next time we have a home game, right Maynard?"

"That's what I'm here for," the taxi man told them with a grin.

As they headed back along the rough gravel road, Morais asked Margo if she'd like to see where he and the others of Santa Nepenthe's middle class lived.

"I'd be honored," she told the man. "Is it far?"

The taxi man laughed at that. "On this island, nothing is very far. How long have you been here now?"

"Oh, you know what I mean," Margo replied as Morais turned left and started back up the hill. By the cathedral, he veered right, as though heading for the royal palace. As they wound their way across the island, Morais explained to Margo that before the Americans landed during the World War, the island had only the royal family and the people.

That navy petty officer, Mayhew, and I were the first, I guess, of what you'd call a true middle class. Mayhew opened his little infirmary and I started my telephone company, then later my cab company.

The Sovereign Hotel was built by US forces as a bachelor officer's quarters and field hospital. When the war was over and the Americans left the island, it sat abandoned and vacant for a few years until Mayhew and I convinced the newly crowned Manny Souza that a hotel would be a plus for an island like ours. We had islanders pitch in to do renovations and fix up and paint the place, then appointed a lady to manage the building. She was an older lady, but then running the Sovereign was a pretty simple task.

"The place had few guests. Who even knew about Santa Nepenthe back then?

"We did get one other writer here back in1956, I believe it was. He wanted everyone to just call him Papa. Hemingway came here to try and overcome the alcoholism that had plagued his life and ruined his health. His wife, Mary, figured it would be nearly impossible for the man to find a drink here. Unfortunately, it was equally difficult to find any intellectual stimulation. The man had a minor nervous breakdown and had to have a special boat evacuate him back to Florida. I don't think he ever mentioned his time on Santa Nepenthe to anyone, surely he never wrote about it."

They were now passing the royal palace without slowing. "Almost there," the cab man told Margo seeing her anxious glance out the window. "Our little village is close enough that we can share electricity and running water with the royal family."

Then, just over a small rise, Margo saw what looked like a sort of an American post World War II housing tract, like the many thrown up for men returning from service. Each dwelling was coated in pastel colors of thick stucco and the roofs were red clay tile. California ranch style came to her mind. There was a row of four houses on either side of the road, and another block of houses on a side street to the south. The houses to the north enjoyed a spectacular view out across the Caribbean.

"Wow," she exclaimed. "This is nice."

"We think so," Maynard Morais smiled. "I'm very happy to live here. And I have my children as neighbors on either side of me."

"On the sea side of the road?" Margo asked. "Naturally," the taxi man smiled, adding "The baker, Carlos, lives directly across from me, Viktor, the head of our football club, lives at one end of the block and at the other end, Gunter has our package store in his garage. He also runs a shuttle service over the Charlotte Amalie when we need it.

"What!" Margo exclaimed, "What package store? You mean like a liquor store? I always thought Sport had the only booze on the island, then I learn the football club has their own supply of beer. Now you're telling me people can just come out here beyond the palace and buy their libations?"

## Chapter Thirty-Four

"Not just anybody can buy from Gunter," Morais told her hesitantly. "I guess you'd say it's kind of a private club… No, that doesn't sound right."

"You mean he only sells liquor to the neighborhood?"

"And the palace, uh, and Vista Para o Mar," the cab man told her with a nod.

"An elitist group, then," Margo frowned, "On an otherwise free and equal island. Where does this man get the stuff, anyway? How did he get into such a business?"

"It's another long slice of island history," Morais told her switching off the engine and turning to face her. "At the end of the war, when the Japanese surrender was announced and the fighting had ended in Europe, the navy boys stationed here on Santa Nepenthe went a little nuts. They all got very drunk and loud."

"And this Gunter person supplied the booze to them?"

"I'm serious here, Margo, please just listen. Gunter wasn't even born yet. Anyway, some of the sailors borrowed a patrol torpedo boat from the docks and went racing circles around the island. They ended up grounded on a sandbar just off the north beach. They raced the engine so hard trying to free their vessel that they blew up the motor. The navy command, in a hurry to leave the island and go home simply left the grounded PT boat there.

"A few months later Gunter's father had a vision. He enlisted two of his buddies to get the boat running again. Old man Moore, the father of the current captain of the Dexter, he brought catalogs from the ship chandlery in San Juan and they figured out what was needed to put PT-162 back in service. That was the start of it."

"Okay, so Gunter's father had a boat. Was he planning on some serious fishing?" Margo looked puzzled.

"No," the taxi man exclaimed. "He'd had a vision. And the priest told him it was nothing less than a message from God. He could elevate himself almost to island royalty by fetching things for the royals from the surrounding islands. Soon he was bringing back shoes and other items of clothing for those who asked him, for a small tariff. He already had a large stash of surplus navy clothes and shoes, so people were used to buying from him.

"Years later, when Gunter himself was a teenager, Gunter started sneaking beer and rum aboard to bring for me and my friends. We would have these bacchanals on the beach. When the father finally caught on, rather than punish his son, Pop started bringing the stuff himself and offering it for sale to a few close friends. That was long before there was Vista Para o Mar." Behind the row of tract homes, the sun was dipping low towards the sea's surface and the sky was lighting up in a bruise of pink and purple.

"I can understand alcohol gaining some popularity," Margo mused. "In fact with the Caribbean so full of pirate lore; I'm surprised Santa Nepenthe didn't start making rum from early days."

"No water," Morais replied simple. "Not enough to grow a decent crop of sugar cane and none to waste distilling the brew. And besides, according to the priest, the first Portuguese that settled here thought it should be a temperance colony. They were a very pious crowd."

"Let me guess," Margo said. "Everything changed overnight when Vista Papa o Mar was built."

"Well, not exactly," the taxi man told her. "Things built slowly for some years. Gunter's father had started ferrying O Cabeça and his bride over to St Thomas to shop or eat fine dinners. Then others requested the service as well. The big change came when commercial cruise ships started pulling into Charlotte Amalie. Overnight all these 'duty-free' liquor emporiums opened up on that harbor. Booze was suddenly cheaper and more plentiful, and with a much large selection."

"Did you and your friends start drinking more?" Margo wanted to know.

Morais laughed. "No, but Manny Souza did. This was about the same time that his, oh, you know…"

"Yeah, and we won't mention the wife again," she smirked.

"When Gunter's father died, Gunter found they had a small fortune tucked away in the bank over on St Thomas. He decided he'd buy a newer, more powerful craft, one that would ride a bit easier in rough seas. Imagine his surprise when the boat dealer over in Charlotte Amalie told him some maritime museum up in Connecticut wanted to buy the old boat. They planned to repaint it as PT-109, the famous boat commanded by President John F. Kennedy for a memorial."

"That was a stroke of luck." Margo gave Maynard a look that said 'does this tale go on much longer?'

"I'm rambling, aren't I," Morais tsked. "You must give a very old man an indulgence now and then. Anyway, after people started moving into Vista Para o Mar, Gunter's business doubled overnight and now he's one of Santa Nepenthe's wealthiest entrepreneurs.

"My neighbors are a nice group of people and all ambitious folk. On quiet Sunday afternoons, after church, we like to sit around and brainstorm about how we might improve our island home… Anyway, I need to get you back to town so you can get ready for your dinner with the royal girls."

## Chapter Thirty-Five

As Margo was exiting Maynard's old Ford outside Sport's bar, she saw Amelia pulling up in a silver C class Mercedes sedan. Funny, she remembered the royal daughter saying she learned how to drive in California, but had no recollection of ever seeing her driving here on Santa Nepenthe. Had the car been parked along the north beach when they'd met and she just didn't notice it? Well, a ride like that would be a hard thing to miss.

The passenger door of the Merc opened before the car came to a complete stop and Miriam was out, throwing her arms around Margo as though they hadn't seen each other in years. She heard Manny Morais behind her call, "Bye Margo, have a great evening."

"I called ahead," Amelia told Margo, getting out of her flashy ride. "Sport should have something good for us."

"I'm ready for one of those martini drinks," Miriam put in, rolling her eyes.

"Have you been driving that all along?" Margo asked Amelia. "I've never noticed…"

"I don't like to leave it at the beach," the royal daughter demurred. "There might be a sand storm and I couldn't stand to see my finish marred. So I usually have one of the guards drop me off and pick me up. But tonight, we're doing things in style. I hope you brought your appetite."

Inside, Sport had prepared a table for them away from the bar. He'd even draped the rough wood surface with a white linen cloth and set out rolled white serviettes. This must be an occasion.

"Are we celebrating the Panther's big win today?" Margo asked, drawing surprised looks from all around her, including Sport.

"I didn't know you followed our local club?" Miriam giggled. Then in a louder voice, "Sport, darling where's my martini? I want a double, with gin and right away."

Amelia patted her hand. "Just sit tight, little sister. You'll get your drink soon enough."

Sport shimmered up to the table wearing a white dinner jacket. Where had he gotten that? And he had a bar towel draped over his arm.

"And what would you ladies like to start your evening?" he asked with a smarmy grin.

"A martini," Miriam blurted out bouncing a little in her seat.

"Shall we all start off with martinis?" Amelia asked, angling her head up at Sport but catching Margo's eye.

"Sounds fine to me," Margo replied.

"Yeah, gin martinis," Miriam added.

"Well, what *is* the occasion?" Margo asked again.

Amelia leaned across the small table, almost eyeball-to-eyeball with Margo. "I spent the entire day with Kennedy. We were designing the posters and handbills he will get for me. He says the first thing he is going to do is erect two ginormous billboards beside the main road, with my face smiling down. They will say, "A. Souza is your best bet – Vote Amelia Souza,' and then, 'For Better Schools, Better Roads and a Better Life.' How does that sound? People will walk or ride by these billboards every day." She then backed up an inch or two out of Margo's personal space.

"Well, that's good for a start…"

"You don't think it will guarantee a win for me? Kennedy says it will really catch everyone's attention."

"Amelia, honey, you don't think other candidates will have clever advertising as well? I'll bet our friend Friend can afford three times as many posters and billboards."

"Daddy won't give him permission to build billboards," Miriam crowed.

"And that would be unfair. *All* the candidates have to have equal access to all the voters."

"You sure about that?" the young girl asked.

"If it's to be a free and fair election," Margo assured her.

Sport arrived with their drinks balanced on a round silver tray to halt the conversation momentarily. When the drinks had been sampled, Amelia spoke, "Well, what more am I supposed to do?"

"You need to go out and meet with the people face-to-face. Instead of going to the beach, you should be going to the school, to the cathedral, to the commoner's marketplaces. You must ask these people what they want and need in their lives, show that you genuinely care about them… and about their children. Show the people that you are one of them."

"But I'm *not* one of them," Amelia stated in a haughty tone with eyebrows raised. "I am a **Souza**!"

"Then someone who can convince them that he or she *is* one of them will win the election," Margo stated with finality, and then asked, "Did you take any public speaking courses at Berkeley?

Amelia was saved from answering by the arrival of the food. Sport brought huge plates of fish and what looked like baked Russet potatoes that must have come from off island. Miriam announced that she was ready for another martini.

There wasn't much talk during the meal, except for comments about what a good repast it was and how excellent a chef Sport had turned out to be. The feral cats, smelling the fish, staged a parade around the ladies feet and under the table as they ate. As the plates were cleared, the tabbies followed Sport back to the kitchen hoping for the scraps. Margo tried to address the issue of reaching the common people again, but the royal daughters kept the topic all girl talk.

"I'm going to die an old maid on this island," Miriam lamented staring into the empty glass of her fifth martini. There isn't a single eligible man near my age in our social class."

"What happened to Game Boy?" Amelia giggled. "I thought you had something going there?"

"Game Boy?" Margo echoed.

"Miriam's neighbor over in the condos," the eldest Souza girl confided. "He's not a bad looking young man, just a year or two younger then sister... But a real twenty-four carat weirdo. He lives in some kinda fantasy world, all dungeons and dragons!"

"Huh?" Margo barked.

"Gerry is a game designer," Miriam defended. "He owns the rights to a dozen or more best selling computer and X-box games and he's creating new ones every day. He's worth oodles of millions, but I don't think he cares that much about me."

"He's sleeping with you in your apartment almost every night," the elder sister ejaculated. "Why do you think he doesn't care about you?"

"Oh, he cares about me alright," Miriam sighed. "I'm like his teddy bear or something, just good for cuddling. And sex," she added in a whisper. He's hiding out here on Santa Nepenthe because he's agoraphobic, he says, whatever that is. He can't stand people, especially crowds of people."

"That doesn't sound so bad," Margo comforted. "You can always count on him being here for you."

"Yeah, sure," the younger girl pouted, "only it isn't even really *me*. He wears these creepy thick black goggles to bed, with little antennas, and when we're doing it, he keeps calling me the names of the princess characters or the witches from his games. I just couldn't see him ever being a proper father or husband. At least your fellah, Amelia, is a *somebody* on this is…"

Amelia was on her feet sending her chair flying backwards. "Shut up, don't you say a word," she screamed. "I'm running for the highest office on this island and I can't afford any scandals! Not another word."

Margo leaned back in surprise, eyes darting from one Souza girl to the other. Sport was immediately at their table. He retrieved the fallen chair and set it up right behind Amelia who slowly lowered herself back into it, still breathing heavily, and drained her martini, looking toward Sport for another.

"I apologize for raising my voice," she told Margo. "My sister would know better, if she wasn't such a booze hound.

"One thing I *did* learn in America is about political scandals. Everybody and nobody seem to be interested in who might have influence on a candidate and who they're sleeping with. I will *not* have that here on Santa Nepenthe." The she drained the fresh martini as Sport put it in her hand.

Margo pretended a huge yawn. "Oh, excuse me. It's been quite a long day. I think I need to get home and grab some sleep." The Souza girls looked at each other and then at Margo. Miriam's eyelids were wavering, but probably as much from drink as from sleepiness.

"Sport, darling, can you put the check on daddy's tab?" Amelia called as the three exited Sport's place. Amelia asked," Can we give you a ride up to the hotel?" To which Margo replied. "I think a walk in the night air would be good for me. See you again soon."

As the Mercedes disappeared around the first bend, Margo retraced her steps bar into the bar.

## Chapter Thirty-Six

"It's Kennedy," Sport told Margo as he reached behind the bar for his special Estonian vodka.

"Huh?" she inquired, parking on her favorite stool.

Sport went through their ritual, setting out two shot glasses and filling them. "Amelia has had a thing going with Kennedy since they were kids. Everyone on the island knows, except maybe old Manny. Thinking about it, yeah, he must know as well. Anyway, it's no big secret and certainly not scandal material."

"And that's what Amelia's big outburst was all about? Seems kinda silly to me." She took a sip of the drink in front of her. "Who would care?"

"The old padre up on the hill might. Remember, the Catholic Church on this island hasn't really changed in four-hundred years. Most people here listen to the priest about what they should do and how they should live day-to-day. Life here is all centered around church and family, if the old guy should pronounce her to be living in sin?"

Margo shook her head and sipped a little more vodka. "You ever go up to the church, Sport?"

The barman laughed loudly. "Definitely not my thing," he told her as he tossed his drink back in one go and reached for the bottle to refill his glass. "As a kid, my parents would drop me off at Sunday school; I'd walk in the front door and out the back where my best friend was waiting along with a couple other guys. We'd go across the boulevard to the Owl Rexall drug store where we'd buy quart bottles of Dad's Old Fashioned Root Beer. Dad's Root Beer came in a brown glass bottle that looked like beer. We'd peel off the labels and sit down on the curb in front of the church to have our refreshment, hoping that passerby's would think we were bad boys drinking beer." He chuckled at his memory.

"Weren't you the naughty boy," she laughed. "I was always the good little Jewish girl. I tried hard to please my parents. I would never have ditched Torah study."

"You probably wouldn't have even spoken to someone like me either," Sport chuckled.

"Oh, I might have," Margo confessed with a faraway look. "I kissed more than one Christian boy on a dare. I even dated a few, but it never got serious."

Sport refilled Margo's glass even though it still had a little liquid left at the bottom. "It would 'a been interesting to have known you back then," he mused.

"Well, that was then, now is now," she told the man with a sideways glance. "So, what do you make of Amelia's chances if she wants to keep that superior attitude?"

"If she was a guy, I think everyone here would be happy to buy into it," Sport stated wiggling his eyebrows. "People have always loved and respected a strong leader."

"A *male* leader, you mean," Margo countered.

"Well, yeah," Sport agreed, "that's what they've always had here."

"So can this superior 'Souza' pose work for a woman? Could it work for Amelia?"

Sport closed his eyes and rubbed his temples.

"Well, could it?" Margo pressed.

Sport poured himself another shot and made to pour one for Margo as well, but her glass was still half full. "Yeah, you've got something there," he confessed. "She's gonna have trouble from the get go just being a girl."

"I rest my case," Margo chuckled, finally knocking back her shot. "Amelia needs my help more than she knows. But I'm not volunteering any more. From here on out, she's on her own unless she wants to come down from her high horse and do it all my way."

While she was talking, Sport refilled her glass. When she was done speaking, he proposed a toast to old Manny and his daughters. Margo quickly knocked back the shot and slammed the glass down on the bar with glassy eyes. Sport was right there and ready to refill it again.

"You're shtrying to get me drunk, aren't sh'you?" Margo asked with a giggle.

"Busted." Sport laughed. "You think this white; not-so-Christian boy could get a date?"

"I don't shacly feel like walkin' up that hill," the lady replied. "I could probably shtay here tonight and we c'a cuddle a bit...But don't try to take advantage of me shust cause I've had, hiccough, a fodka or two."

Sport came around the bar, carrying the half-empty bottle, on wobbly legs. He closed and locked the big warehouse doors, put an arm around Margo's back to ease her from the barstool and help her up the back stairs. They made slow, drunken love, dozed for a few hours and then made love again. Neither was all that consumed with passion, just a pair of old friends seeking a little 'feel-good' pleasure.

"So do you think you and I could become, ah, an item?" Sport asked early in the morning, propping himself up on his elbows to look down into Margo's eyes.

"Well," she replied, suddenly serious, "You live a sort of Peter Pan existence," the lady had acquired a certain hard set to her eyes, "running a bar in a Caribbean banana republic. I, on the other hand, have a very comfortable career with a well read and award winning newspaper back in New York. I'm a serious minded woman, Sport. I don't mind a little dalliance here and there along the way, but I'm certainly not ready to cash in all I've worked for to finish up on some tropical island as a beach bum, no matter how nice it might seem to be right now. But while we're at it, could we try this one more time?"

## Chapter Thirty-Seven

Margo's novel had been progressing nicely since the political furor had died down a bit. Emmanuel Souza had, a few weeks back, made the formal announcement that elections would be held in June, which one would have thought might increase the tension, but instead it seemed to have a calming effect. At least for Margo, life returned to a more normal pace.

Posters and yard signs had begun to appear for both the major candidates and a few other island wanna-bes as well. Carlos Mendonça, the town baker, advertised that he would be well qualified, as did one or two other lesser-known islanders, but the majority of the campaign handbills proclaimed either, "Vote for A. Friend," or "A. Souza is your best bet – Vote Amelia Souza." The Supreme Leader had stated with finality that there would be no billboards erected on his island. They might be useful in the short run, but would they set an ugly precedent for the future? Once they were up, who was to stop their use beyond the election to sell tobacco, deodorant or other modern things?

Margo was busy typing and Sport was washing mugs and glasses when Captain Moore of the Dexter came running through the doors all out of breath. Margo looked up to see, behind the man, the ship's crew was busy constructing some kind of long ramp at an angle from the vessel's deck to the pier.

"Can you call Morais?" the captain half shouted to Sport. "I've got his delivery for him. He has to sign for it."

Sport picked up the telephone but when he connected, Morais said he knew nothing of any delivery. He had ordered nothing from off island in a month or more. "I will, however, come down, have a beer and check it out," he told the barman.

When Sport had hung up the phone, Margo nodded her head towards the wharf outside. Sport wiped his hands on a bar towel and came around to the front of his café. He and Margo both stared as one of the Dexter's crew eased a large silver van down the ramp, directed by First Officer Clemmons. Another crew member was approaching Sport's place with a mail sack.

The short Philippino sailor, Abang, withdrew a letter from the postal bag addressed to Maynard Morais and marked U S Priority Mail. "Is señor Morais here?" he asked. At that point the old Ford was just pulling up outside. Sport tipped his head toward the doors in answer to the man's question.

Morais entered in a bit of a stew. "What's this about a parcel for me," he demanded of the waiting sailor.

"It's more than just a parcel," Captain Moore laughed. The young Philippino extended his hand that held the letter. Morais tore open the envelope, unfolded the single sheet of paper and reached in the breast pocket of his Hawaiian shirt for his reading glasses. The man's lips moved slightly and his face clouded as he poured over the words. He finally looked up, shaking his head.

"It seems that Senhor Friend is attempting to bribe me or to buy my vote. He says he is giving me as a gift a newer and better vehicle for my taxi service, but I never asked to own such a vehicle. His letter says that, when he is our leader, he will provide a fleet of such vehicles so that I may employ many drivers to serve his properties with taxi service. I'm not sure what I should do at this point." He slipped his glasses back into his shirt pocket.

"Don't look a gift horse in the mouth," Sport chuckled. "Does the letter say anything about there being strings attached?"

"It says that this new taxi is to be mine and I may keep it even if he, Friend, should lose this election," the taxi man said. "But I have my doubts…"

As Morais was speaking, the silver van rolled up on the wharf and was parked beside the man's old Ford cab. First Officer Clemmons climbed out of the driver's seat and came through the warehouse doors. "I've got some papers for you to sign, Maynard," he told Morais.

The taxi man retrieved and donned his spectacles once more. Clemmons held out a stack of forms to the taxi man. Morais backed his bottom onto a bar stool and started reading. Sport placed a cold draught at Morais' elbow then offered Clemmons and Moore drinks while they waited. Margo already had a half-finished beer in front of her, but she seemed to have forgotten about her computer open on the counter next to her drink.

"In order to take possession of this new vehicle," the taxi man said, still very much focused on the papers in front of him, "he says I must surrender my old Ford." Then disdainfully he added, "He calls my old and faithful friend an eyesore, the nerve!" The man continued to turn over page after page on the bar top before he finally raised his head and replaced his glasses in his shirt.

"How about we go take a gander at this new ride," Sport suggested. "Let's see if you like the look of it."

It was a late model Dodge Caravan with two leather bench seats behind the driver's compartment and plenty of storage area in the rear. The van's side door slid open at the push of a button. The tail gate was also powered so that no lifting was required. "This bus must have cost many, many American dollars!" Morais proclaimed. "It would take me years to pay for such a machine."

Margo glanced at the rear of the van over Morais' shoulders. "It even has a New York license plate that's good for a few more months, so it isn't brand new." She didn't know why, but Margo made a mental note of the van's plate number, New York NAB-1740.

Sport opened the driver side door and glanced in at the dash. "Only twelve-thousand miles on the clock," he noted, "So practically new."

"I just don't know," the taxi man pondered.

"How about we take it for a little spin up through the foothills," Sport told him wiggling his eyebrows in Groucho Marx fashion. "If you like the way it handles?"

Morais climbed into the cab and looked around, familiarizing himself with the vehicle's peddles and gauges. "It has an automatic transmission," he mumbled to himself. "That would be good for my aging knees."

Sport went into the warehouse and returned with his crudely scrawled 'Back Soon' sign which he taped to the doors just before he closed and locked his bar.

Sport, Margo and the officers from the Dexter all piled in and Morais started the engine. He drove slowly through the three blocks of Cidade Sebastian, then gave the throttle a bit more of his foot as they climbed the first rise out of town. Margo could see a smile spread across the man's face in the driving mirror.

"I guess it would be a good thing for the island," Morais said meekly as he passed the Santa Nepenthe cathedral. "And it would be here to serve us even after Amelia wins the election," he added in a soft voice. "I'll need to move my radio over from the old Ford before I send it back with you, Captain Moore."

Margo expected Friend to be waiting when they returned to Sport's place, standing there to gloat over his big bribe, but the man didn't show. As Sport reopened his doors and proposed they all drink a toast on the house, to the islands new taxi cab, the black Mercedes pulled up beside the new van. It was, however, Friend's lieutenant, Johnny, who exited the dark vehicle.

"I'm here to collect the papers for Mr. Friend when you've signed them," he told Morais, then he went to a booth in the back corner and sat waiting. Sport poured shots for everyone, even offering one to Johnny, but Friend's henchman declined. Morais tipped his vodka back and then concentrated on the stack of papers that Johnny had come to collect.

"My boatswain is pretty handy with electronic things," Captain Moore offered. "Shall I have him transfer your radio over while you're doing the paperwork?" he asked the taxi man.

## ❧ Chapter Thirty-Eight ❧

That night, back in her hotel room, Margo kept thinking about that New York license plate on the back of Morais' new taxi van. She had written the number down on a cocktail napkin when they returned to the bar as it was already bothering her at the time. Now, the more she thought about it, the more it nagged at her. Something just didn't seem right about the whole transaction. Some guy who hadn't yet won the election giving some old islander a sixty-thousand dollar gift out of the kindness of his heart? No way.

The next morning, even before making coffee, Margo sent an email to one of her colleagues at the Trib. Joshua was the paper's major crime reporter and had lots of good contacts with the police, both state and local. In her message, she asked if he could do her a big favor and check on New York plate number NAB-1740. That done, she started her morning coffee, humming a little tune to herself and decided she would walk down the hill to Sports for some breakfast.

Margo packed up her laptop; maybe she could even get some writing done sitting on the pier side bench outside Sports. It was too nice a day to stay indoors.

Sport prepared a lovely soufflé with lots of cheddar cheese and some hot peppers one of the islanders had given him in payment for a drink. She carefully picked out bits of egg and cheese without peppers attached to feed her tabby friend that shared her space at the bar most mornings.

Margo was about to close her computer to take it outside when a little bell sounded to tell her that she had mail. She opened her e mail program quickly to find a response from Joshua at the Trib.

"What do you know about this license number!" he had written all in capital letters, then in regular type, he continued, "Cops have been looking for the van that belongs to this plate for over two months. Silver Dodge van disappeared from the parking lot of a shopping mall on Long Island. Please advise. J"

Margo clucked her tongue and shot a wide grin at Sport. "Well, now we know where the island's new taxi comes from," she chuckled. "Seems that someone stole it on Long Island."

"Uh-oh," Sport frowned. "What do we do now?

"Well," Margo mused, "as Santa Nepenthe has no diplomatic agreements with the US, no one is likely to come looking for it here, even if my friend at the Trib that gave me the news tells them where they might find it."

Morais had entered the bar while Sport and Margo had their heads together. "Stolen," he wailed. "I'm driving a stolen van? And I gave my own car away? What the hell am I going to do? I'd better go up to the cathedral and ask for a lot of forgiveness."

"I wouldn't worry about it," Sport told the man. "It'll be Friend's karma and not yours."

"Karma?" Morais queried, "What is karma?"

"Take too long to explain," Margo told the man. "Something to do with God holding the real thief responsible and regarding you as an innocent bystander." She thought for a moment, then added,

"You might want to take the New York tag off the van though and throw it in the sea."

To Maynard Morais' down face, Sport told him, "The people's insurance back in New York have probably bought them a brand new van by now anyway."

Margo clucked her tongue, "Well, this certainly gives us a little insight into our, ah, Friend. I can't wait to tell the Souzas about this one."

She sent an answer to Joshua's email telling him she had seen unlikely tourists driving the vehicle on St Thomas and had been suspicious. "Thanks for the favor," she typed, "might alert police about someone smuggling cars to the Virgin Islands." She was careful not to mention Santa Nepenthe. She knew no one would show up here searching. The insurance company would choose to write the vehicle off rather than go through the expense of locating and returning the van from such a distance.

"So have you had any fares since you acquired the new car?" she asked Morais.

"I'll be taking the Souza girls to the beach shortly," he answered. "Maybe you'd like to join them? It's a perfect day out there."

Margo gave it a long, hard think. "Well, I *was* planning to get some work done today..." she mused. "But, on the other hand, I should let Amelia know the news about Friend being a car thief."

"You're sure the Souza's will not take my van away as stolen property?" Morais said with a look of concern.

Margo laughed. "I doubt if they'll give it a single thought. Amelia has more important matters on her mind right now."

After a light lunch, Margo loaded her own beach chair into the back of Morais new van, just in case the girls weren't expecting her. The sisters were surprised and very happy to see her when the big Dodge pulled up by the sand.

"Kennedy is working on getting me foreign aid," Amelia greeted Margo along with a wave. "He also says that the main bank he uses for the island in America is thinking about offering us a line of credit based on the gold we own."

"And hello to you, too" Margo laughed. "That's good news for your campaign. So how have you been? I've noticed your signs and posters all around the island."

"Those were Kennedy's doing as well, if you'll remember. He's a very smart man."

"Father came up with the slogan," Miriam put in. "Father is very clever too."

Kennedy says that right now I'm a few votes ahead of Friend according to the people he has polled. And he says I've got plenty of time to win more of our people to my side.

"Oh, where are my manners, would you care for a glass of wine?"

Margo nodded and accepted the glass Miriam filled for her. After taking a sip, she told them, "I just may have some information to help you. That new van Morais is driving? Did he tell you that it was a gift from Friend? Some kind of bribe I suspect, to buy Maynard's vote."

"No!" shouted Amelia, "Shut up!"

"That's just what it is. Friend brought it here and insisted Maynard surrender his old car before he could have the new one to make sure Maynard couldn't go back to his old taxi."

"That's really playing dirty," Amelia said with a hard look. "He knows I can't afford to give away big gifts."

"But that's not the best part," Margo continued, her hands clasped before her. "It wasn't Friend's van to give! It was stolen by the man's buddies in America, stolen and then shipped here. The New York police are still looking for it."

"But Friend hasn't left the island all year," Miriam put in. How could he arrange such a thing?"

"He can do plenty using the Internet," Margo assured the sisters, "or the telephone. The point is he has some very powerful people helping his campaign. I think organized crime in America wants the hotels and casinos on Santa Nepenthe, it isn't just Friend. He's just a front man for some very evil people."

"That's quite a story," Amelia said taking a big drink of her wine, "but it's pretty farfetched. Have these people even seen our island? How would they know anything about us?"

"The Internet again," Margo told them. "But besides that, they really don't need to see Santa Nepenthe. All they need to know is the island's size and location. With that information, they can make plans and calculate how much money such a place could bring in for them. They'll figure they can tempt gamblers from Puerto Rico and the American Virgin Islands as well as vacationers from all over America. They're probably already counting the money they'll make…"

"*If* they win the election," Amelia stated emphatically. "First they have to win the election. Do you think Friend will have enough stolen cars to buy everyone's votes?"

## Chapter Thirty-Nine

Margo was sitting in Sports a few weeks later when the news came that Viktor, the coach and owner of the Panther's Football Club, had managed to arrange a match between the island team and the world renowned West Indies Football Association, the Pirates. Local gossip going around hinted that setting up such a match had cost a great deal of money and that money had come from one of Santa Nepenthe's candidates in the upcoming election.

In a rare appearance at the waterfront bar, Viktor had defended himself to Margo stating that a game against a team known all around the globe would be a very positive thing for the island's young players. And anyway, the only strings attached were that Friend be allowed to address the fans at half-time to express his support for the Panthers. The off-islander had even hinted that, when he was elected, he would build a new, modern stadium that would be the envy of all the surrounding islands.

"I must attend that match," Margo had told Sport when Viktor left. "I think I might even call Maynard today and reserve a seat in his taxi."

"Whatever," was the barman's disinterested reply.

"It does seem this man is spending an awful lot of money to win this office."

"Yeah, an investment," Sport lamented. "You've said yourself he stands to pull billions out of Santa Nepenthe if he gets his way with these casinos."

Skoot Larson

A group of locals had stopped in for a beer and were seated just down the counter from Margo. One of these Nepenthens, overhearing Margo's conversation, turned his head to her and Sport. "We will work for this Friend person... building his hotel or his airport, but only until we have enough money to buy a fifty foot Landry fishing boat." The islander smiled a great grin as his buddies' nodded agreement. "Then we will quit and become our own bosses. We will go out every morning to catch fish or shrimp, then in the afternoon we will go over to St Thomas and sell the bounty that the sea has given us in the fish market for American dollars."

"Aren't you worried that this man is a crook? That he's likely to destroy your island?" Margo asked the group sincerely.

"My family has owned our little farm here on Santa Nepenthe free and clear since the days when pirates sailed these waters," a second local from the group told her. "We don't really need sewers or fancy air conditioning units, but money to rebuild our house would be nice. We pay our small bit of tax to the government each year, always on time. Friend cannot take this land from us. Let the tourists have our beaches and their gambling. It will give the rest of us more money to spend. At least we will have a *man* in charge."

Margo shook her head. She guessed that it would be pointless to argue with these voters. Then she saw Morais' van pulling up out front. "Sport, give Maynard a beer on me when he sits down," she told the bar man, then called excitedly, "Hey Maynard, just the man I was hoping to see. Come sit with me."

"You were looking for me?" the taxi man asked.

"Yes," Margo told him. "I've just heard about this big football match with the West Indies. I want to book a seat in your taxi van to the game."

"You and a few dozen others," Morais kidded. "But of course, Margo, you know that you can always ride with me. Your shotgun seat in my van is forever reserved, as long as you will sit with me at the match and keep me company while I watch my grandson play."

"You've got it, Maynard. So have the Panthers ever played the West Indies before?"

"Are you kidding?" the taxi man responded. "The West Indies Football Association is so far out of our league... But it should be an interesting match. Our guys are really fired up, practicing hard. Just playing this team will bring our standing up in our own league."

They talked on for some time about football and politics. Margo bought Maynard another couple of beers and Sport set him up a couple free shots. The locals finished their drinks and headed back up the hill to their families. Sunset found Margo once more with a strong alcohol buzz and no more work to show on her novel.

Sport offered more free shots while dropping hints that maybe they should have another hot night together, but Margo's mind was somewhere else.

Friend, she thought, not content to just offer stolen vans as election bribes, was now paying for impressive football shows. How else was he planning to buy this election? Next thing you know, he'd be throwing money into the crowds to buy universal support. Wasn't there anything that Manny Souza could do to reign in this craziness?

But the Supreme Leader didn't want to show favoritism. He truly believed his daughter was strong enough to overcome whatever the opposition could throw at her. Should she, Margo, try to schedule another audience with the O Cabeça and explain things to him in simple terms that even an old man with an eighth grade education could understand?

But no, the man had a lot of pride. He would never listen. And why was she playing Crusader Rabbit here anyway? She would be going home to New York soon, finished novel or not. While coming to an unspoiled island to write had seemed a great idea when she was sitting in her office back home, the reality had turned out to be something totally different.

Maybe there was no perfect place to write a novel. Many of the great works in history had been written in cramped garrets, in lonely studio apartments or even, like Jack Kerouac, in a speeding car racing across America.

Well, she still had a few months left of her sabbatical time. That swift bolt of creative energy could still strike. She would just have to try harder, spend less time boozing and schmoozing.

# ❧ Chapter Forty ❧

The day of the big match arrived to find the entire island abuzz with football. It became the number one topic everywhere, dwarfing election talk in its huge shadow. As the island taxi drove along the roads to pick up the fares that had reserved a seat in the van, they passed crowds of people walking along the highway. In spite of ninety-degree heat, many were wrapped in scarlet and blue Panther scarves. Margo had never seen so many baseball caps on any one day, definitely not so many in Panther team colors.

João and Claus were the first into the silver van after Margo. Morais then crossed the main highway driving east almost to Vista Para o Mar, where he jogged north on a scrubby dirt track to what looked like a fallen-down old Victorian mansion. Maynard got out of the van and walked to the building's front door which hung just a little crooked in its frame. The man knocked and three very well dressed women opened the door and filed out, a mother and two teen-age daughters by the look of them. The mother turned back to the door and shouted, "John Boy, we don't want to miss the kick off. Get a move on your fat butt."

The family took the full back row of seating and the taxi van moved on, making the now familiar turn to the long pair of ruts that led to Reggie's house of packing crates. With Reggie on board, Morais aimed his fully loaded van for the stadium. The area behind the cathedral was one solid wall of human flesh in scarlet and blue.

Viktor, the team owner and coach, stood near the edge of the green pitch. When he saw Margo and Maynard, he waved them over and led them up the bleacher steps, parting the crowd in his path. At the top, there was a row of empty seats with a blue ribbon stretching its length labeled 'reserved.'

Maynard thanked Viktor and motioned for his party to take the saved seats. Apparently, it was a package deal that included cab fare and an excellent view of the game. In front of the stands, more fans crouched down, while additional spectators lined the areas behind both goals. Margo couldn't believe the size of the crowd.

Across the field, the mass of people parted and the teams poured forth. The faces, arms and legs of West Indies men stood out very black against their bright white jerseys and sky blue shorts. They jostled with the Panther players, all fun and games. Margo could sense that the visiting Pirates were expecting this to be a walk in the park after all the highly skilled professional teams they regularly played.

Only minutes after the kickoff, however, the Panthers took possession of the ball and managed to keep it throughout most of the first half. Morais' grandson, Jacob tried for three goals, the first two being blocked by the Pirates' very agile goalkeeper, but the third slipped past the man's lunge for it. The stadium went nuts as the Panthers achieved the first point of the game.

The one-nil score on the board drove the Pirates into a fury as they realized what they were up against. Their man Churchill, lucky number 7, showed a paroxysm of activity as he took possession of the ball and tried time after time to get past the Santa Nepenthe goalie, right up until the halftime whistle sounded.

# Friend

As the teams left the pitch, four young men rolled a small raised dais toward the center of the field. Once in place, they chocked the wheels and walked off while a black BMW drove onto the grass.

Alphonse Friend, dressed in a tan, summer-weight suit, Panama hat and dark glasses, made his entrance, walking slowly to the improvised podium. When he arrived, he removed his sun glasses, shaded his eyes with his left palm and took his time swiveling his head from one bleacher to the other, as though making eye contact with each individual in the stadium.

Friend briefly turned away from the microphone, cleared his throat, then brought his head back around, ducked slightly and spoke in his heavy Hoboken accent. "Most 'a you folks were born right heah on this wond'aful island," he began. "I bowt my home heah ovah ten years ago, so I ain't a native but I feel like I am one 'a you. And like all 'a youse, I want to see Santa Nepenthe grow and prosper… Ent'a inta the twenty-first century like the oth'a islands that surround us and the rest of the big world out there. I want you all to have the economic power to buy the many things you see every day on television and the Internet. I sincerely want to help you all realize these dreams, to provide education for your children and a hospital facility for when you might get sick or injured."

The crowd remained fairly quiet. Was it because folks were listening intently? Or were they listening at all?

The man went on. "In ordah to make these dreams real, I would like to bring prosperity to Santa Nepenthe, to bring jobs, good paying jobs, to Santa Nepenthe. As your elected leader, I will do just that. I will build an airport, so modern goods may be brought to you. I will build hotels and casinos that will bring tourist to Santa

Nepenthe, tourists with money to spend to make our island rich. And where there are tourists, there are abundant jobs; hotel and restaurant staff, fishing guides, card dealers and security people to keep order.

"But even before there are hotels or casinos, there will be high paying positions for the men who will work building these things. I will see that many of youse are trained to operate the bulldozers, to pour the concrete and to craft the furnishings that go into these structures. For those who don't wish to learn new skilled trades, there will be plenty of construction jobs wielding saws, hammers and nails. There will be a job for each individual, no mattah what your skill level might be.

"And so I urge you on Saturday, June the fowth, to go to your polling place and vote for A. Friend." He paused for effect, then repeated Vote for prosperity. Vote for A. Friend."

The man stood back, searching the stands and waiting for cheering, applause, something, but the crowd was quiet. Thinking fast, Friend shouted, "And I will build youse a new stadium that will be the envy of all the otha islands. God bless the Panthers!" At this, he received the ovation he'd been seeking, but it was disappointing that his audience cared more about their football team than the big promises he'd just made. The BMW convertible drove back out across the grass to collect him and Friend disappeared from the area. The people had expected that he would at least find a seat on the sidelines and watch the game.

# Chapter Forty-One

The second half of the match was the fastest, most intense game of football the islanders had ever seen. The West Indies had vowed that they would not be shown up by some tiny island most of them had never even heard of. The referee almost wore out his yellow card tracking aggressive behavior that went beyond sportsmanship. Both teams were able to score a goal, but in the end Santa Nepenthe won the match 2 – 1.

The club sold out of Red Stripe beer in the last ten minutes of play which left the team store scrambling. Viktor located Gunter in the crowd and they entrusted the keys to the package store proprietor's old Toyota to one of his clerks, commissioning her to bring whatever bottled beer she might find in Gunter's refrigerator and bring it fast.

Sixty-three odd assorted bottles of beer arrived moments after the end of the match and sold out quickly to jubilant fans. A few fans had whiskey bottles that were passed around, but there was no trouble, no fighting or arguing. Everyone was just exceedingly happy that their own, home-grown team had beaten a very popular team with a heavy reputation. Friend's little campaign show was totally forgotten in the celebration of Santa Nepenthe's mighty Panthers.

Maynard, Margo and company had a slow walk back to the island's taxi van, moving only as quickly as the shoulder-to-shoulder crowd would allow. The pace didn't improve after Morais got the van going. He tooted his horn, but it had no effect on the happy celebrants. Even out on the highway, the people walked and danced three and four abreast, reluctant to break off conversations to let the vehicle pass.

The side roads were more open when they turned from the main road to drop off passengers, but then returning to the highway proved almost impossible.

Margo eventually arrived back at Sports only to find the place packed. Sport had moved her stool back behind the bar to hold her place. When she came through the crowd, the barman carried the high chair back out where he offered two customers a free drink if they'd clear enough space for the lady to squeeze her stool in. Morais was able to work his way in beside her.

"Friend made a big speech at halftime," she told Sport with a wink and a grin. "He promised everyone jobs and money."

"No one else has mentioned it," Sport remarked, pulling Margo and Maynard draught beers, then adding, "Damn, this keg is almost gone. You think you could come back here and watch the bar while I get one from the back and change it?"

Margo laughed. "I think your customers will allow you five minutes. Everyone seems pretty happy in here."

"Yeah, well," Sport frowned. "This is getting to be too much like work. And I'm going to be short a few items until Wednesday when the Dexter returns. Remind me to get on the horn first thing Monday and call Puerto Rico to double my usual liquor order."

"Hey, you're making money and you're complaining?" Morais reminded him.

Sport grinned. "Point taken," and he reached beneath the bar. "At least we've got plenty of my special poison. I don't know about you, but I'm ready for a shot before I wrestle that heavy keg in here. The three buddies each downed a shot, Sport changed out the empty firkin and they all had another shot of vodka. The crowd was now all singing the Santa Nepenthe national anthem, swaying gently back and forth. A few drank up and departed, others ordered more booze.

Around four in the afternoon, the familiar black BMW convertible pulled up on the wharf. Johnny got out and went around to open the rear door where Friend emerged, still wearing his light tan suit. They entered the bar, Johnny walking a couple paces behind and to the right, tensed up and waiting should anyone try to hurt his boss.

Friend walked through the crowd with his hand extended, but no one broke from their conversations about football to shake with him. After one lonely circuit of the room, the off-island candidate elbowed into the bar and turned to face the crowd.

"Hey, you all know me. It's A. Friend. I want to be your next Supreme Leader." He looked around, but few had raised their heads to acknowledge him.

"I want to buy everyone here a drink," Friend shouted, which *did* get the crowd's attention. The celebrants pushed in towards the bar, someone elbowing Friend out of the way which almost earned the man a punch from Johnny, but the press was so thick, the little hood couldn't get his arm up and straight.

The football fans collected their free drinks and returned to their conversations. Friend made another smiling walk through the crowd with his hand extended, but only received the odd 'thank you' as he progressed. When the free beer had been consumed, fans began to depart the tavern en masse, leaving the two Jersey hoodlums sharing the room with Margo, Maynard and Sport. Sport presented the bill.

"Just put it on the man's tab," Johnny said flippantly, but Sport shook his head 'no.'

"I afraid I'll need cash this time," Sport replied, addressing Friend.

"Aw, shit," Friend barked. "Pay the man, Johnny."

The lieutenant peeled of a couple large American bills from a thick roll and slapped it into Sport's palm with an angry face.

Sport smiled back at him. "Thank you for your custom, Mr. Friend. And good luck with the election."

Johnny left a stripe of tire rubber on the wharf outside as Friend's BMW pulled away.

## ✿ Chapter Forty-Two ✿

**W**ith the election now less then a month away, rumors started circulating that Friend was willing to buy the votes of any Nepenthens who were still undecided, and even some who might want to change sides. Margo also heard that Amelia had finally begun a campaign outreach directly to the island's common people.

"Apparently, with her poll numbers slipping, our favorite royal daughter went to the cathedral to seek the priest's blessing for her campaign," Morais told them one afternoon in Sports. "The old padre pretty much told Amelia exactly what you had counseled months ago, that she needed to show the people she was one of them. He told her that the name Souza meant nothing special in the eyes of God, who viewed all his children as equal. After that, Amelia decided that she had better pay attention to the man of God and began driving around the island looking for groups of folks she could speak to one-on-one."

Later in the week, Amelia stopped by Sports herself to thank Margo for the advice she had been so late in taking up. "The ladies I speak with all tell me I've got their vote," the royal daughter crooned. "The men, however, are a different story. They ask tough questions like am I ready to go into battle to defend Santa Nepenthe, which is silly because Santa Nepenthe has never ever fought any kind of battle. A few have actually suggested that I should choose a husband and then let him lead the nation, as men have always done.

"But a few listen to me and give me a chance." She turned to Maynard Morais, "All the men who are your neighbors out beyond the palace have had encouragement for me. I think I still have a chance. And I believe, when it comes right down to it, many of these men who mock and criticize me being a woman will vote for me in the end because I am a Souza."

"I'll drink to that," Margo told her, giving her shoulder a sisterly pat.

"And I'll join you in that drink. I'll even buy the first round," Amelia announced, then turning to Sport, she said, "Will you join us in a double martini?"

"Do you think there'll be room in there for all three of us?" Sport joked as he set up an assembly line of glasses with olives and began the search for his martini shaker.

Margo explained Sport's bad joke to the royal girl while the barman shook the individual drinks and poured them out, the royal daughter first, then Margo. He mixed his own last, after serving Morais. Margo noticed that Sport filled the shaker for his drink and hers from beneath the counter, most likely using his private Estonian stash rather than gin.

On their second round of drinks, they were distracted by a ruckus out on the pier. Friend's BMW pulled up where the wharf met the boardwalk, a small crowd of island men following. Johnny had a bright red bullhorn, through which he was repeating over and over "Vote for A. Friend. Friend will bring money to Santa Nepenthe!" As Johnny spoke, Alphonse Friend leaned over the car's door passing out Gourd notes to any man who would shake his hand, then tipping his Panama hat like an organ-grinder's monkey to the money's recipient and saying something. They couldn't make out his words at such a distance, but the man was probably thanking them for their promised votes.

"Pathetic," was Margo's instant response, "How could anyone stoop so low."

"I'm sure it's been done often throughout history," Sport cackled. "Probably even back home in America… Chicago and New Jersey come to mind."

"And our, ah, Friend is from New Jersey. Okay, point to Sport. But do you think they'll vote for him just for a handful of Gourd?"

"Don't forget the promise of more money, big bucks," the bar man replied, "Unfortunately, this island isn't home to a lot of geniuses but we do have a few that are hungry, especially hungry in the abstract, like for toys, fast cars and other status symbols."

When Friend had driven away, a handful of his audience members came into the bar to spend the easy money they'd just received. With a few Gourd in hand, they wanted whiskey, not beer. The islanders pushed some tables together in the back corner and proceeded to get drunk as they spoke of the fast cars and speed boats they would buy when Friend's big money came to Santa Nepenthe. At one point, Sport had to don his army jacket and threaten the group in order to stop a fight in progress. After that, he cut the men off. "You've had enough whiskey for one day, he told them.

"That's okay," the hothead who'd been ready to fight told him. "We've already spent all of Senhor Friend's money for today. Maybe we'll be back when he gives us more."

"You think the man is gonna buy your vote more than once?" Sport asked.

"He already has," another of the men laughed. "To that stupid monkey, we all look the same." The whole group roared with mirth at that statement.

When Morais came in for a beer a few days later, he reported seeing a similar scene up by the football stadium. There had been a handful of men, all volunteers, making repairs to the bleachers when Friend pulled up and started passing out Gourd notes. "The men had all lined up and taken his money," Morais told them, "then when the man drove away, the workers all headed for the Panther team store. They'd totally forgotten that the store was still out of Red Stripe from the match against the West Indies. I think in the end, Viktor promised to buy them a couple bottles of whiskey but not until the repairs to the stadium had been completed.

"The work was finished in record time," Maynard laughed. "And the whiskey Viktor sold them wasn't exactly cheap."

## ☀ Chapter Forty-Three ☀

When the morning of May third rolled around, sightings of Friend throwing out money to potential voters had died out, in fact his campaign had become strangely quiet. It was exactly one month before Election Day, a time you would expect his campaigning activities to be doubled.

Amelia had become a tireless speaker, making daily appearances all over the island. The Saturday before, she had hosted a bar-b-que at the stadium, feeding a few hundred families; men, women and children, while she spoke to them of bringing both a hospital and a high school to Santa Nepenthe.

"I will be asking America for aid money to build our land into a better place. We don't need foreigners in large numbers coming here to gamble, clogging our roads and beaches. We may invest in some limited tourism, inviting people from afar to come enjoy our beaches along with the natural flora and fauna of Santa Nepenthe. And we will build slowly, as a united people, creating jobs on our own terms."

The crowd was paying attention to the Souza daughter, cheering in the right places. "With limited tourism, we can have jobs for fishing guides and for park rangers as well, men and women that can show off our natural beauty to those who choose to visit Santa Nepenthe. The main thing is that we have a better stronger Santa Nepenthe, not for off-islands to despoil but for our own people to enjoy."

Now, three days later, the island was still talking about Amelia's bar-b-que and what a strong, focused impression she had made. Maybe a girl could have the ability to lead. The royal daughter was gaining rapidly in the polls and without offering bribes to any of her constituents.

Morais had stopped into Sport's early for lunch. Margo had her laptop open on the bar, but was once again doing as much drinking as writing. "Things are coming together in my story," she told Sport and the taxi man when they asked. "From this point, I can relax a bit and take it easy. I think I'll wait until I'm back in New York to do my final read-through and edits. Amelia's surging ahead in the election polls here has really put my mind at rest."

The three ate burgers with steak-cut fries while listening to sea birds call and the distant crash of waves along the south facing beach.

Morais excused himself to go pick up a fare, leaving Margo and Sport to hang out in the otherwise empty bar. When Sport had cleared the counter, he reached beneath the bar for his Estonian vodka.

"You really believe Amelia has this sewed up?" Sport asked.

"Well, she's doing a great job of reaching out to the people. And it almost seems like Friend has crawled under a rock and given up. Has anyone seen him in the past week?"

Before Sport could answer, the island taxi pulled up discharging a handful of senior off-islanders from Vista Para o Mar. Morais parked the van then followed them in. "Bird Watcher's Club luncheon," he announced to Sport. "Sorry, no one gave me advance notice of where they wanted to go so I could have let you know."

"Not a problem," Sport grinned. "Would you folks like a big table? I can push a few smaller ones together for you." Morais went back out and drove his van away.

There were six of them, two natty old gentlemen in ascots and blazers and four ladies in very old party dresses. The men both wanted single-malt Scotch to start. Three of the ladies asked for double Piña Coladas. The last member of the group demanded a frozen margarita.

A Piña Colada sounded good to Margo. "While you're mixing those coconut drinks for the ladies, could I get one as well?" she asked Sport. The barman gave her the first one he mixed. "Cheers!" he told her.

The rest of the drinks were quickly mixed and dispensed and Sport took the group's food order. They all wanted the catch of the day and rice pilaf which made it simple for Sport. While he was preparing their dishes, the island taxi returned with a single fare, a frail and thin gray-haired lady who was dressed more in the fashion of a bird watcher in jungle khakis with a pair of binoculars around her neck.

"You who," she called to the crowd at the table, "you could have waited for me." She turned to Margo and Sport and confessed, "I had a sharp-shinned hawk, Accipiter striatus, sitting on my railing. I *had* to get some photos of it but this lot was hungry and couldn't wait. Could you send a vodka gimlet over to the table for me? I'll just eat what everyone else is eating.

Out beyond the coral reef, Margo noticed a ship heading for the harbor of Santa Nepenthe. "Do we have a delivery scheduled today?" she asked Sport. Without looking up from the margarita he was mixing, Sport replied, "Wednesdays and Fridays. The supply ships from Puerto Rico come on Wednesdays and Fridays. You should know that by now."

Margo ordered another Piña Colada, sipped it slowly and stroked the tabby cat that sat in front of her on the bar top as she watched the approaching gray vessel. She asked Sport for some boiled local shrimp as the vessel neared the dock. Margo was running her last shrimp through the cocktail sauce when the ramp was brought from the vessel's deck and green clad soldiers began to pour forth onto the wharf led by an overweight man in a white ice cream suit and dazzling Panama hat. The soldiers, carrying nasty looking machine pistols, quickly fanned out along the waterfront.

Sensing a story, Margo fished through her purse for her old press credentials. She rushed out the door and ran up to the man in the white suit. "Margo Drelve, New York Tribune," she shouted, half out of breath. "Can you tell me what's going on here?"

With his nose in the air and a condescending glare in his piggy eyes, the man replied, "Isn't it obvious? We have come to build the airport."

"With soldiers?" Margo asked in a confused tone.

"The soldiers are only here to conscript laborers," the man replied.

"But they haven't held the island's elections yet," she cried. "The people may not want an airport. We won't know until the people have spoken."

"There will be no elections," the white clad man told her.

"And you're *conscripting* labor, not hiring them?"

# Friend

"When the airport plus a hotel and casino are up and operating, bringing in a profit, we will consider *hiring* some of the brightest and most loyal," he told her. "As for now, our idiot friend running for the office of island leader here has given away too much of my money but produced too little in the way of positive support for our project.

"But the labor will be paid?" she asked with a voice full of concern as she scribbled quick notes on her spiral bound pad.

"They will be fed and sheltered. That is all I can promise until the casino brings us a profit." With that, the man turned back toward his troops signaling that the interview was finished.

# Part III

# Run for your lives!

## Chapter Forty-Four

Margo walked slowly backwards away from the fat man in the white suit until she was sure he wasn't paying any attention to her movements. She then turned around and bolted for the large double doors of the bar.

Sport saw her running toward the warehouse entrance and stopped work on the drink he was mixing to watch her. Margo entered the bar looking terrified. "Sport, we've got to get out of here. Right now!"

"I've got a few customers in the place at the minute. When they leave I'll come with you."

"Sport, you don't *understand*," she told him in a loud hiss. "Those soldiers out there on the pier? They've come to take over the island for Friend. There isn't going to *be* any election, there is going to be a coup d'état. We have to leave right now."

"But I'm a major in the island army. Shouldn't I stay and help our men fight them?"

"You and all the able bodied men on Santa Nepenthe wouldn't stand a chance in hell against these thugs. They're armed to the teeth. Come *on*, we've got to get out of here now."

"And my customers?" Sport asked.

"Just leave them to their drinks. Serve what you just mixed and let's go."

The barman brought a vodka gimlet to the gray haired lady who had come into town from Vista Para o Mar for lunch then returned behind the bar. He shed his apron, grabbed his special vodka bottle from under the bar and took Margo's hand. Together they casually walked out the back door of the warehouse then slowly strolled up the hill toward the Sovereign Hotel. At the first bend in the road, they cut down the alley behind the butcher's shop then legged it into the scrubby desert-like brush that bordered Cidade Sebastian. Margo's intention was that they should look like lovers in search of a secluded place to lay down their blanket and make love.

As they topped the first rise that would conceal them from the formation of soldiers that lined the wharf, she urged Sport on to a faster pace. Sport took a long drink straight from the vodka bottle and offered it to Margo as they ran. "Later," she panted. "I'll be ready for a drink as soon as I feel safer."

They made their way into a small jungle and then east over the rocky hills sprinting for a hundred yards or so and then slowing for awhile to catch their breath. So far, they hadn't seen another soul out in the badlands.

Just as they reached the top of the rise, the afternoon showers struck with an intensity neither could remember in recent history. Sport grabbed Margo's hand and led her to a patch of jungle just off the trail. They cowered under the leaves of a squat banana tree until the downpour ceased.

In the light sprinkle that followed the cloudburst they continued on, both soaked to the skin, wet clothes clinging to their bodies that the tropical sun soon dried to simple dampness. After about an hour, Vista Para o Mar came into view.

"Where are we going, anyway?" Sport asked when he saw the gates of the condo community.

"Right there," Margo told him tipping her head toward the gated complex.

"Someone in Vista is going to help us?" Sport sounded confused.

"*We* are going to help us," Margo stated emphatically. "There's an unguarded yacht harbor at the foot of the bluffs. We need to steal one of those boats and get to St Thomas where we can get help from the Americans."

"Wait just a cotton pickin' minute," Sport hollered, stopping his forward progress. "I can't go to St Thomas. I'm a wanted man in the US."

"Stay here and you might be a dead man," she told him through clenched teeth. "Now let's get down there and find a boat."

Sport started to raise the bottle to his lips again. Margo stopped him with a look. "You won't be any use to either of us drunk," she barked.

"Have you ever seen me drunk?" Sport laughed.

"Have I ever seen you in fear for your life?" Margo countered. Sport dropped the now half empty bottle into the deep computer bag that still hung from Margo's shoulder. As he did, a thought struck him.

"Your novel." He exclaimed. "You've left your computer with all your work on it back on the bar."

"And if we're lucky and can get help in time, maybe I'll get it back one of these days. No novel is worth my life at this point."

They reached the fence that enclosed the rich folk's condominiums and started toward the sea along the wrought iron parameter. Sport glance through the bars quickly. He grabbed Margo, breathing, "Oh shit."

Margo followed his gaze to find the fat man in the Panama hat from the docks reading something from a clipboard to Friend just inside the fence from them. Margo tackled Sport and they rolled a few feet closer to the bluff.

"Did he see us," she hissed.

"Uh, I don't think so, Sport told her with a foolish grin. "They were pretty wrapped up in whatever they were talking about."

"We had better assume that they *did* see us," Margo thought out loud, "and be extra cautious."

"Can I have my bottle back?" squeaked Sport.

"No, you may not," Margo stated emphatically. "Do you know how to get down to the marina?"

"There's only the two stairways at either end of the terrace that run along by the apartments," Sport told her, then he closed his eyes in thought.

"But I seem to recall Morais telling me that when his kids were young, long before my time here, they used to play in the cove where O Cabeça had those boat slips built. He said something about a trail a short way to the south."

# Friend

Margo was already steering them in that direction, walking hunched over to present a smaller target should someone be watching. Sport frog marched behind her.

They found the trail about half a mile away, crumbling earthen foot holds carved into the face of the cliff. The pathway was sheltered from Vista Para o Mar by a lava outcropping extending almost to the white sand below. As soon as they'd taken ten steps, they were able to stand upright, which made their descent both quicker and easier. One step halfway down crumbled beneath Margo's weight but Sport caught her wrist, held fast and eased her down to the next foothold.

Arriving on the narrow beach, they took off at a fast trot for the marina, which appeared to be deserted. The board fingers of docking were protected from the outside world by chain link rather than pike-headed iron posts. Both Margo and Sport were over the wire within seconds and crouching to creep along the floating boards.

Sport pointed to an aging Chris Craft. When Margo followed his finger, she noticed that the ignition keys were dangling from the dash on the boat's bridge. They nodded to each other then crawled on their bellies along the dockside. They were almost to the boat when a familiar voice behind them said, "Hey, what are you guys doing here?"

They looked around to see Amelia's form towering over them.

Sport emitted a low groan but Margo jumped up and threw an arm over the royal daughter's shoulder.

"Amelia, I haven't got a lot of time to explain, but your life may be in danger. You'd better come with us. I'll explain later."

At this, Sport stood also, flanking the royal daughter, and with Amelia between the two of them they walked up the boat's gangway. The motor turned over on the first try. Sport didn't even bother to undo the mooring lines, he simply threw the engines into full reverse, jigged the tiller around and then slammed the throttle full forward, taking a portion of the dock with them as they roared toward open water. The slats of docking came loose from the mooring lines when they entered open water.

"My God, what are you doing?" the royal child protested. "This is Mr. Cohen's boat. Where are you taking me?"

Margo heard someone yelling from the distance and turned to look at the condo community, fearful that Friend or his fat buddy might have seen their departure, but she saw only a very old and wrinkled man in a blue blazer and boating cap standing high up on the development's terrace waving his arms and shouting.

"That's Mr. Cohen." Amelia shouted.

When the tip of Santa Nepenthe disappeared over the horizon, Margo retrieved Sport's special Estonian vodka bottle from her bag and took the first drink before she passed it to the barman at the wheel.

## Chapter Forty-Five

When they'd each had a couple drinks from the vodka bottle Margo turned to Amelia. "I apologize for grabbing you so abruptly," she told the girl. "But I think it's very lucky for both of us that we ran into you at the marina."

"I was just feeding my fish," Amelia replied in a fearful voice. "There's some tropical fish that wait for me there every day and I bring them some pieces of bread…"

"Listen, Amelia," Margo interrupted. "An hour or so ago a ship landed at the port by Cidade Sebastian, a ship full of soldiers. Friend brought these soldiers to take over Santa Nepenthe. He's not waiting for an election, he's assuming power now."

"Oh my God," the girl said again. "What about father? Do you think they'll kill my father?"

"I hope they don't," Sport shouted over his shoulder. "I really like old Manny."

"Amelia, don't worry about your father. I think the first thing they intend to do is to round up all the able-bodied young men. They're going to force the men of Santa Nepenthe to build Friend's airport for him. They probably won't bother your father. They most likely don't want your dad to know they're on the island. But we'll have to get help fast to stop them, before they decide to take the palace."

"And my sister?" the terrified girl cried out.

"We just have to pray that she's safe," Margo told her.

It was nightfall when they reached the harbor at Charlotte Amalie. Sport had no idea where he should tie up the stolen Chris. Margo hailed a bearded young man passing close by them in a Hobie catamaran. "Is there a public dock nearby?" she shouted. The man ran fingers through his bright red beard and moved his head in the direction from which he was coming. "You're headed straight for it," he shouted back. "Ten bucks a night, twenty five if you need hook-ups."

Margo and Amelia went out on the deck and retrieved the sodden rope lines that they had been dragging all the way from the Vista Para o Mar marina. The lines were heavy with water, but together they managed to wrestle them onto the boat so Sport could tie them to the moorings. One rope still had a deck cleat and a piece of docking tangled in its far end which dropped off into the harbor when Margo jerked the line aboard.

When the Chris Craft was secured to the public dock, the three went off in search of the local Coast Guard station. The people they passed in the streets were friendly, smiling and helpful. "Just down from the Legislature building on the waterfront highway, you can't miss it," a very old, black and thin man told them, "It's right by Fort Christian." He pointed them in the right direction and they set off walking at a rapid pace. Sport thought about hailing one of the colorful taxis that kept driving by them, but they didn't have any American dollars to pay for the ride.

They reached the Coast Guard station just after nine in the evening. A mere boy in a blue work uniform stopped them at the station's gate to ask their business. Margo and Sport both started talking excitedly at once. Amelia stood back from them wringing her hands.

"Whoa," cried the young man, "One at a time. Is it an act of terrorism you wish to report? Where are these armed soldiers?"

"Santa Nepenthe," Margo pleaded. They're invading Santa Nepenthe."

"And where is that, ma'm? Is it on the other side of the island? I'm kinda new here."

"No, it's the next island to the northwest," she pleaded. "You've got to help."

The guard looked confused. "I think I'd better call my watch commander," the young sailor told her, ducking back into his kiosk. The man picked up a telephone receiver from the desk and talked for a long time. He seemed to be getting switched around to a number of different people before he snapped to attention and barked "Yes sir!" into the instrument. When he hung up, he turned to Sport and Margo to say. "Captain Taylor will be here shortly. He's the CO of the entire Virgin Island's Coast Guard group."

A pair of Coast Guardsmen that looked more like military policemen escorted Margo, Sport and Amelia through the gate, then marched them into the station's administrative building, up a flight of stairs and to a large conference room where they met Captain Taylor. The captain was in dress whites and had another man in the uniform of a lieutenant commander along with two enlisted men seated around him at a long oak table. He stood when they entered and shook hands with his three guests from Santa Nepenthe.

"I understand you came here to report that someone is invading one of our neighboring islands," the man began as the trio was seated. "By the way, this is Commander Jacobs, the CO of the St Thomas station." The other officer gave a slight bow.

"And then we have Radioman Cartwright and Yeoman Harrington. They'll be taking notes and recording our conversation if you don't mind."

All three of the islanders nodded in unison that it would be alright.

"First, for the record," the captain said, "can you each state your name and address?"

Margo quickly identified herself, giving both her island address at the Sovereign Hotel and her Brooklyn apartment that she had sublet for her year away. The captain's eye next traveled to Amelia who in a shy voice told him she was Amelia Souza, the daughter of Santa Nepenthe's Supreme Leader. "My formal address is the Royal Palace," she told the officer, "but I actually reside in Apartment Seventeen, Vista Para o Mar, on our island's east shore. We don't have street addresses on my island," she added.

Sport appeared to grow smaller when the captain's eyes turned his way, fearing someone might remember his long ago run-in with these same authorities. He cleared his throat a few times then squeaked, "Uh, I'm, uh, Patrick Sportacus. I live above the waterfront bar in Warehouse two on the Santa Nepenthe docks." He blinked rapidly as he watched for any sign that his name might ring a bell with the officials, but no one gave him a second glance.

"Now, can one of you tell me what happened? I just want one of you to be the spokesperson. If that person misses a point or gets something wrong, one of the others of you can raise a hand and we'll call on you to make the correction for the record. Who'd like to tell the story?"

Friend

Margo raised a bold hand. "Sir? I'm a journalist back in the states. I'm a reporter for the New York Tribune, so I think I would probably the best qualified to report for you."

Margo told the story while her cohorts gave the occasional nod of agreement. She carefully explained that the island was planning a free democratic election in June, just five weeks away. When she described the soldiers pouring forth from a ship on the island's waterfront, Amelia's eyes grew moist.

Captain Taylor stopped Margo at this point. "Can you describe this man in the white suit that brought this army to your island more fully? Did anyone call him by name?"

Margo did her best to elaborate. As she was speaking, the captain made a note on his pad, tore the top sheet off and handed it to the radioman, whispering something to the man that they couldn't catch. Petty Officer Cartwright jumped up, saluted and immediately left the room.

When Margo had finished the tale, including how they had found Amelia on the docks at the marina and had escaped, the Coast Guardsmen all left the room briefly. When they returned, Cartwright, the radioman, was with them again.

"I want you to come with me," Captain Taylor told the island trio and turned to leave the room. The two petty officers took up a position following Margo, Sport and Amelia as they left the room.

The captain and commander led them up another flight of stairs with a wide door at the top. Through the door they could hear a loud whine and a flopping of something in the air. When the portal was opened, they saw a white helicopter with a wide red stripe across its nose, rotors spinning at full tilt. The commander gestured toward the bird and the petty officers gave them each a hand up through the cargo doors.

"Where are you taking us?" whimpered a fearful Amelia.

"US Navy Command at Roosevelt Roads," the commander told her. "That's on Puerto Rico, it's less than an hour flight time from here.

## Chapter Forty-Six

The helicopter landed just after two a.m. at Roosevelt Roads. Four sailors in what looked like battle dress met the flight and escorted Margo, Sport and Amelia from the landing pad to a waiting gray HumVee. One of the men tapped the roof after the trio was belted into their seats and the vehicle sped off on a well lighted two lane road. No one spoke to them throughout their ride.

The military vehicle pulled up at a loading dock behind a large yellow building. Their unsmiling sailor guards opened the Hum-Vees' rear doors and helped them slide out and then walked them up the ramp and into the building. Without a word, they were taken to another large room and seated at a less impressive table. This table was painted gray and covered with a scarred slab of Formica.

Looking around, Margo noticed there was a large sheet of Plexiglas at the front of the room with the outlines of all the northern Caribbean islands; a sort of transparent map. Someone had circled Santa Nepenthe and St Thomas in grease pencil and there were curving sets of arrows to the north west, near the island of Cuba. A number of desks around the perimeter of the room were occupied by navy men seated before computer screens and wearing headphones.

Her attention was drawn from the board at the front by a door opening in the rear of the space. Captain Taylor entered the room along with a full navy admiral, two navy captains and a pair of men in dark gray suits with very short hair. One had a dark red crew cut, the other, closely cropped salt-and-pepper waves.

"Welcome to Puerto Rico," the admiral said in a soft voice. "I apologize for the abrupt manner in which you were brought here, but your discussion with the Coast Guard in St Thomas has raised considerable interest in some areas. Before we begin, my name is Admiral Stone, my colleagues here are Captain Davies," one of the navy men gave a slight bow, "Captain Nelson," the other navy man put a hand to the bill of his cap in a mock salute, "and agents Crabtree and Smyth from the Central Intelligence Agency. The shorter of the G-men with the gray hair gave a weak smile while the other's lips just seemed to twitch a bit.

The admiral continued, "I'm sorry to ask, but can you tell your story once more Ms. Drelve? From the top?"

Margo began her tale again. When Friend's name came up, the taller G-man's lips twitched once more. "I think his real name is Alphonse Ameche," she told them, causing the two suits to look at each other and nod slightly.

"This Ameche guy," the shorter government man asked, "He lives on your island?"

"He bought a condo from our government five years ago," Amelia put in, "A retirement condo. He's been living there all year round. Not like the folks that only come in the winter when it's cold in America."

The two men looked at each other again. The tall one said, "That's where he's gotten off to. I'd a never guessed. Another big question answered."

His partner replied, "Now if we can take him into custody."

"What's he wanted for?" Sport asked.

"Oh, murder for a start," the shorter man said, "tax evasion, extortion… we've got quite a list."

The admiral signaled for Margo to go on. When she got to the part about the piggy man in the white suit that landed with the soldiers, the red head in the dark suit moved his laptop computer along the table so it was in front of her. "Do you think you could recognize this man? I'd like you to look at some photographs and tell me if you recognize anyone."

On the laptop screen were six portrait type photos of unsmiling men. None of their faces registered so Margo shook her head. The man rolled a mouse ball and six more faces appeared.

"Uh, I think that's the man, left end of the bottom row," she said, cocking her head to one side. She squinted at the screen and the man in the suit held down a pair of keys until the face Margo had chosen filled the screen.

"Yes," she exclaimed. "Yes, that's him."

"The Zipper," the suited man said to his partner. "Carlo Zeppo. I was wondering what he's been up to lately."

"Thought he'd retired to Sicily," the other suit chuckled. It was the first time either of their faces had shown any sign of life.

Margo gave them a confused look, but the man said, "Continue your story please. The second suit motioned the navy admiral over to a corner where the two held a quiet conversation of their own. When they were finished with their sidebar, the admiral left the room.

By the time Margo had finished *her* tale, the Admiral had returned. He came over and stood before the island trio.

"We'd like to help," he said in his soft-spoken tone, "but your island doesn't have any formal diplomatic relations with America." He focused his eyes on Amelia. "You say you are the daughter of the island's leader?"

"Yes," Amelia perked up. "I am next in line for the throne if something should happen to my father." She said proudly.

"And your father has scheduled democratic elections for next month?" the first G-man asked, "so your people can freely choose if you will be the next leader or if someone else might be better?" The girl nodded.

The other dark suit then asked, "Amelia, do you have the authority to enter into agreements with other nations?

Amelia's face clouded momentarily, "I guess so... I mean sure I do. I'm the *first born* daughter."

"And would you be willing to sign paperwork that would establish a diplomatic relationship with the United States of America?" his gray haired partner asked. "If you can do this, our American navy would gladly step in, drive these gangsters from Santa Nepenthe and we'll monitor your elections for you to see that they are conducted fairly and proper. I also see in your file that you've submitted a request for foreign aid. Once you've established a diplomatic link with America, we'll be able to put this on the fast track."

"What the man is saying," the admiral put in, "is that if you enter into a pact with America, we will have to come to your island's defense."

Amelia turned a questioning face to Margo, then Sport and back to Margo. Both shook their heads in the affirmative and Amelia brought her eyes to the two men in the suits.

"That is what I came here to do," she told them with a grin. "So you will save my people? You'll protect my father and sister?"

At that, a female sailor entered carrying a sheaf of papers bearing official seals.

"If you could go over these documents with me, Ms. Souza?" asked the red crew cut. "I'll show you where you need to sign and where to initial certain paragraphs."

She looked around to see the admiral had a telephone in his hand and was making fresh grease-pencil arrows on the glass map.

One of the captains came over and leaned down to the trio of islanders as Amelia flipped pages and scrawled her name on the appropriate lines.

"You're very lucky." He told them. "We just happened to have a navy task force starting an exercise off Guantanamo Bay. One aircraft carrier, three destroyers and a landing ship with two companies of marines. They can be off the coast of Santa Nepenthe by late afternoon, but we've scheduled a fly-over of fighter planes right after dawn to put your invaders on alert.

## Chapter Forty-Seven

The battle to take Santa Nepenthe back lasted less than an hour. Most of the hired mercenaries threw down their guns as soon as the US Marines appeared on the docks. A few ran for the hills and tried to hide among the locals, but the people of Santa Nepenthe were not having any of it. Two men had shucked their uniforms and pulled damp washing from a clothesline to try and disguise themselves but were quickly revealed as neither could speak a word of Portuguese, the official second language of the island that every school child learned early on.

The destroyer Halsey, DDG-97, patrolling off the east coast of Santa Nepenthe, noticed two men dressed in white dragging heavy suitcases down from the terrace of Vista Para o Mar. The ship's captain ordered the tin can to get as close as they could to the condo's marina while they kept a close eye on the two men.

The suspicious pair tossed their bags into the cockpit of a sleek, black cigarette boat on the marina's outer landing and fired up the powerful engine. They roared out of the small sheltered dock area trying to steer well to the destroyer's rear quarter. As they rounded the ship's fantail, they found themselves face-to-face with a small launch filled with sailors bearing riot shot guns and M-16 automatic rifles. The thinner of the two suspects jumped overboard and tried to swim back towards the marina but was pulled down by his fancy wing-tip shoes and his white silk suit. His partner put his hands in the air. When the sailors came alongside the speedboat, the man was already shouting that he wanted his lawyer. A. Friend was unceremoniously dragged aboard the Halsey with a long boathook.

The second wave of marines to land by Cidade Sebastian heard loud pounding coming from both the closed and padlocked bar and the adjoining warehouse that flew the flag of Santa Nepenthe. A gunnery sergeant brought a set of bolt cutters from his pack and snapped the locks that held the warehouse doors fast. A few hundred island men were huddled inside. Bowls of water and meat were lined against the walls, where the men were expected to eat like animals. It was the same in the warehouse owned by Sport, except that a few men had borrowed bottles from Sport's stock and were crying and drinking, sitting with their backs against the bar.

"They treat us like animals," one man wailed drunkenly, recognizing his rescuers as US Marines. "They were going to make us build an airport for them, working all the day in the hot sun."

Outside, four of the marines cleared the soldiers and bystanders from a section of wharf while their sergeant spoke into a radio on his shoulder. Minutes later, a navy blue helicopter with dark tinted glass set down in the open space. Agents Crabtree and Smyth stepped from the whirlybird's cargo bay, hair un-mussed by the rotor wash and their dark suits looking freshly pressed. The G-men found their way to the marine platoon leader who directed them to a HumVee that had been lowered onto the pier. The agents climbed into the back seat to confer with the marine contingent's commanding officer.

By evening, the Halsey had tied up at the Cidade Sebastian pier. Their two prisoners, in hand cuffs and leg irons, were turned over to the CIA men who had emerged from the CO's HumVee. A pair of navy MPs lifted Friend and The Zipper into the helo and chained them to an eye-bolt on the airship's floor. Smyth and Crabtree climbed in behind the prisoners while two navy guards stood at attention against the helo's rear bulkhead, preparing for the flight to a federal lock-up in Miami, Florida.

Sport was heartsick at the state in which they'd left his bar, but decided tomorrow would be soon enough to begin the clean up. He was about to go upstairs to bed when a squad of jar heads came to his door.

Oh my God, he thought. They *did* remember me and my little drug run. What have I done? "No good deed goes unpunished," he mumbled to himself, ready to surrender.

But the platoon sergeant came forward smiling, with his hand extended. "Mr. Sportacus?" he asked.

Sport gave a hesitant "yeah?"

"The captain says it's a shame how those guys trashed your bar. He sent us to see if we can put things in order for you, sweep up the broken glass, pick up the litter, and all."

Sport broke into a huge smile, "Uh, yeah, of course. Hey wow. Can I get you guys some beers while you work? Or something stronger?"

Einstein peered cautiously through the tall doors as if asking 'is it safe to return yet?'

The next morning the marines organized a parade through Cidade Sebastian and up over the foothills to the football stadium in order to celebrate Santa Nepenthe's liberation. The two secret agents had confiscated Friend's Mercedes and his BMW convertible along with freezing his assets world-wide. One of the navy captains suggested that Amelia might borrow the beamer to lead the parade. Maynard Morais would be her driver and two companies of marines and a formation of sailors would follow. The Navy Fourth Fleet Marching Band would provide music and a marching cadence from somewhere in the middle of the assemblage.

The word got out quickly. Islanders were two and three deep lining the parade route; newly freed laborers, their neighbors and their families joined by most of the expat residents of Vista Para o Mar. Looking at the happy, admiring crowd lining the route, Amelia knew she would have no problem winning an election here. And when she did, she would take the advice of those nice men from the American CIA and organize some kind of legislature where all the people of Santa Nepenthe, her people, could have a voice. And to express her *own* voice, she would have Kennedy Morais by her side as her consort.

# Epilogue:

# Happily Ever After…

## Chapter Forty-Eight

Six months has passed since Carlos Zeppo, the Mafia boss behind Alphonse Friend, attempted to invade and take over Santa Nepenthe. As it turned out, Sport's worries about America still seeking to arrest him for his drug running all those years ago were little more than a waste of mental energy. In the eyes of American law enforcement, his buddy, Jared, had paid their debt to society for both of them. Besides, it had been a long time ago, beyond the statute of limitations for such crimes.

Sport's cousin, Margaret, had seen the television coverage of the American rescue of Santa Nepenthe on television in Oakland, California, recognized her relative and immediately called the family attorney who *was* looking for Sport. The island barman's father, a San Francisco bay area real estate mogul, had died three years earlier leaving a substantial sum of money to his only son, if said son could be located. He also promised a ten-per-cent finder's fee out of that inheritance to whoever might locate his wayward boy child.

And on this particularly lovely autumn afternoon, Margo was sitting in Sport's bar, all her luggage packed by her side as she waited for the M V Dexter that would take her to Puerto Rico on the first leg of her journey back to New York and her job at the Tribune.

Margo and Sport were saying their farewells in rather loud voices in order to be heard over all the construction noises from the rear of the old warehouse.

"You know you could come back to New York with me," Margo told him. "Margaret told you that no one is looking to kill you anymore."

Einstein, the bar's resident tabby, hunkered down into Margo's large straw purse as if to say, "Me, take me with you!"

"Yeah, I know," Sport replied. "She sent me all those newspaper clippings about the shootout in Nogales. The guys that were after me for the drugs I ditched all died in a matter of minutes, so if I want to go home, I don't have to be looking over my shoulder. But, you know, after sixteen years I've kinda grown to love this place.

"Besides, I'm a local hero here. And right now I'm the biggest single employer on the island, at least until they get my hotel built. Three stories tall, two-hundred-twenty rooms with my original place here as bar, restaurant, and official island historical landmark number one!"

"The renovations in the bar look fabulous," Margo assured him, "Just the right mix of original pirate background and Danish modern furniture. And you say the cruise ships will start coming to Santa Nepenthe sometime in April?"

"I believe we're right on schedule," Sport told her. "Think you might fly down for the hotel's grand opening? Ms. Hix is going to manage the hotel side for me, but only after she takes some course over in St Thomas on modern hospitality."

"I wouldn't miss it," Margo laughed. "In fact, I've already sent out feelers to let me write the exclusive coverage for Time and Newsweek. You gonna give me a discount on my room?"

# Friend

As Margo shouted this last sentence, the room became deathly quiet. Margo glanced at her watch; five-o'clock. Another institution she had told Amelia would be necessary was labor unions and those unions were very strict about working hours.

Einstein hopped up on the bar and touched noses with Margo then rubbed his head along her cheek. "Don't you love me?" his green eyes seemed to say. "Why aren't you taking me with you?"

Outside, an island taxi van pulled up, driven by Maynard Morais himself, which was unusual these days as the taxi company now employed four young men as drivers. The American representatives who visited to monitor elections back in June had offered Morais a Small Business Administration loan backed by the US government to expand his business. The Americans wanted to insure there'd be enough cabs and drivers to chauffer the diplomats that had business on Santa Nepenthe.

"Good, you're still here," he greeted Margo. "I want to buy you a drink before you leave us and thank you for all you've done for Santa Nepenthe."

Margo's cheeks showed a hint of blush as she said, "I didn't do anything special. It was simply my nose for news kicking in."

"But your quick thinking saved us all," Maynard Morais reminded her, "grabbing this big lug barman and high-tailing it to St Thomas to alert the Coast Guard. And you were a big help in getting the island our elections as well."

Amelia had won the election against a young islander who ran on the 'Men Rule' party. She later picked her opponent to be one of her deputies. The island also chose two representatives, the baker, Carlos Mendonça, and Viktor from the football club, from the middle class and ten representatives from the ordinary folks of the island as Santa Nepenthe's new legislature. She appointed her sister, Miriam, as ambassador to America, getting her enrolled in a college in Maryland to earn a four-year degree while she was stationed in Washington DC.

Now, as Sport was shaking a gin martini for the taxi company owner, Amelia's silver Mercedes pulled up next to the island taxi and the new Supreme Leader came into the bar. She was dressed kind of island formal in a long gown of Hawaiian shirt fabric covered in toucans and bunches of bananas, and rhinestone sling-back sandals with a small silver tiara in her light brown hair. The lady walked straight to Margo and gave her a tight hug. "I'm so sad to see you going," she said with a sigh. "I'm really going to miss our days at the beach." Then the royal lady glanced sidewise at the bar and exclaimed, "Oh, gin martinis! Sport, be a dear and fix me one as well."

"So what's new up at the palace?" Sport asked as he went into his juggling routine with the martini shaker.

"Well," Amelia grinned, "for starters, we voted unanimously this morning to proclaim the Sebastian Hotel historical landmark number two. We've allocated funds for a complete renovation and then we plan to turn the building into the Santa Nepenthe State Museum as soon as your lodgings are ready and open. Maynard has promised us a few of the original telephones to put on exhibit. Have you got any old junk around here that we should put on display?"

"I'll have to give that some thought," Sport told her. "I'm sure there're a few trinkets worth donating. Maybe some of the original blue ballast bricks I'm knocking out of the back to connect to the hotel. And I think there's a rusty old cutlass around here somewhere. It could be the very weapon that killed the pirate that brought us our gold."

Amelia laughed, "If you can find that sword that would be the icing on the cake.

"Oh, did I mention we also voted to start work on an airport? Not a giant thing like Friend had planned, just a simple landing strip that can accommodate smaller commuter planes along with a two-room terminal. Gunter is looking into one of those small business loans to buy a pair of nineteen seat planes to start Santa Nepenthe Airlines between here and Miami. That will be good for your business, Sport," she said with a wink at the barman. "Is my martini ready yet? I'm dying of thirst."

"Speaking of thirst," Margo chimed in, "have you chosen a company to build the desalinization plant yet?"

"We've narrowed it down to three," Amelia told her. "The legislature is carefully studying each of the bidders. The deal we want is for the company to build and run the plant but also pay for it from the water they sell to the island's population. The rates have to be reasonable enough that everyone can afford fresh water."

Captain Moore's voice came booming from the doorway. "I hear we're having some kind of party here this evening. Ms. Margo, we've fixed you up a special suite on the Dexter to take you to San Juan tonight and at a discounted rate as well."

Amelia gave the man a questioning look. "I thought I requested that Margo's accommodations be put on the royal tab?"

Moore gave a sheepish grin. "Well, yeah, that's what I meant. I'm just throwing in some upgrades, no extra charge."

First Officer Clemmons and the entire Dexter crew filed in behind the ship's captain. "So let's make with the drinks," Boatswain Abang shouted. "We can't hang around here all night."

Sport brayed a fine bit of laughter and said, "You'll have to get in line. We've had a few arrivals ahead of you including the Supreme Leader of this rock."

As toasts were raised and drinks slammed down, Sport put out platters of local shrimp and cuts of fried area fish for appetizers along with pastries from the local bakery. He hated to see Margo go, but in his heart he knew that they had established a bond across time and would always be close, no matter how many miles separated them.

At two in the morning, when Captain Moore announced that they had to weigh anchor and sail from the island's shores, Maynard loaded Margo's bags into the rear of his silver van and announced free rides out on the pier to the MV Dexter for the entire crew. Margo's island adventure was ending, but a whole new life for the island of Santa Nepenthe was just beginning.

# About the Author

Skoot Larson is a native Los Angelino, a musician, music critic and a Viet Nam veteran. He has also worked as a disc jockey, actor, speech therapist, stand-up comedian, behavioral counselor and streetcar conductor. His previous works include the Lars Lindstrom Zen-Jazz Mystery series, a black-humor novel about health care in America entitled "Apollo Issue," a political humor novel, "The Palestine Solution," a religious comedy, "The Testament of Jessica Crystal," and three previous Dave Holman mysteries. Skoot lives with his two cats in Rockport, Texas.